The Hyacinth Spell

*Also by Frances Y. McHugh
in Large Print:*

Emerald Mountain
High on a Hill

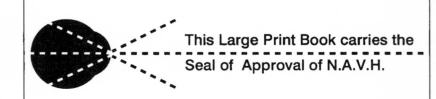
This Large Print Book carries the
Seal of Approval of N.A.V.H.

The Hyacinth Spell

Frances Y. McHugh

Thorndike Press • **Thorndike, Maine**

Published in 2000 by arrangement with
Maureen Moran Agency.

Thorndike Press Large Print Candlelight Series.

The tree indicium is a trademark of Thorndike Press.

The text of this Large Print edition is unabridged.
Other aspects of the book may vary from the original edition.

Set in 16 pt. Plantin by Al Chase.

Printed in the United States on permanent paper.

Library of Congress Cataloging-in-Publication Data
McHugh, Frances Y.
    The hyacinth spell / by Frances Y. McHugh.
        p.   cm.
    ISBN 0-7862-2797-4 (lg. print : hc : alk. paper)
    1. Witchcraft — Fiction.   2. New York (State) — Fiction.
    3. Large type books.   I. Title.
    PS3563.C3685 H93 2000
    813′.54—dc21   00-042571

The Hyacinth Spell

Chapter One

It was a long, tiring trip on the bus from the city up to Lake Tranquil in upper New York State, and when I finally got off the bus in the town of Pinecrest, which was where the boat was to meet me to take me over to the Randolph place on the island of Sanctuary, I was more than glad to feel the clean, bracing, unpolluted air in my face. I took deep breaths of it as I stood and looked around me at the calm waters of the lake, the mountains in the distance and the boats gently rocking at the pier just across the road.

The bus stopped in front of the big inn facing the lake. Doug, my boss, whose place I was visiting, had told me that one of the servants would pick me up there and take me to the island in one of the launches. But I was surprised to see Luke, the chauffeur, jump out of a motor launch, tie it up to the pier and come over to me. I had thought he was down in the city.

Luke was a nice-looking man in his early thirties; tall, broad-shouldered and well built. He had kindly brown eyes and un-manageable taffy-colored hair which he wore rather more close-cut than the present style. His features were large but well arranged, and his smile pleasant.

When he saw me standing at the foot of the inn steps with my two suitcases at my feet, he grinned and waved, he was wearing dungarees and a turtle-necked sweater, both a medium blue, and he looked more rugged than he did in the black chauffeur's uniform he wore in the city. Crossing the road, he said, "Hi, there. Have a good trip up?"

I said, "Yes. It's a pretty ride after you get through the tunnel and away from the city."

He picked up my bags. "This way," he said, heading back to the launch. "The only way to get to the place is by boat. Know how to handle one?"

"Only a canoe and a rowboat."

He laughed. "I'll have to show you how to handle a motorboat. You may want to get off the island by yourself once in a while."

"I doubt it. But I'll try anything once."

"That's not always a good idea. There are some things you are better off not trying." He had reached the launch, which had the name "Ariadne" painted on the side. Jumping down into it, he put my bags on the deck, then held out a large, strong, sunbrowned hand to me. "Watch your step," he warned as I stepped from the pier into the slightly rocking boat. "Do you swim?"

"A little."

He started the motor, untied the boat and said, "You better sit down."

I sat down on a seat that ran along the side by the railing, and he sat up front so he could steer.

I looked around as the boat turned and headed down the lake. Or maybe it was up, I didn't know. I had heard the lake was ten miles long and had several large islands in the center of it on which the very wealthy had summer places. Anyway, it was a beautiful place, and as the boat cut through the water Luke began to tell me who lived in the houses we were passing. Each place seemed to blend with the landscape, and each had its own boathouse with two, three and even four boats. Luke explained, "Every family has several boats, because the life here is on the water, and for those who live on the islands the only way to get to the mainland is by water. All provisions have to be taken over by water as well as everything else, including people."

"Sounds like fun."

Luke shrugged. "It's different, anyway. And of course no one stays on the islands in the winter. They are strictly summer re-sorts."

"And very beautiful."

The motion of the boat was making me sleepy after the long trip up on the bus, and I couldn't suppress a yawn. Seeing it, Luke said, "You'll have time for a nap before dinner. And your room is off by itself, so nothing will disturb you."

I took a deep breath of the clean, clear, fresh air. "But I don't want to waste time sleeping. I'm sure there is too much to see and do."

"Not on the island of Sanctuary. Back on the mainland, there's the inn and a movie and some shops down on the main street. That's about all." He swung the boat across the lake and pointed it toward an island with a group of cottage-like houses running from the shore back to a wooded section. "That is the Randolph place over there," he told me. "The island, as you know, is called Sanctuary, and as they, or rather he, owns the entire island, that's what the place is called."

I said, "Yes, I know." And that was about all I did know about Sanctuary. Doug seldom talked about his personal life in the office so, although I knew about the place, I did not know any of the details. Whenever

Doug was going up there he would just say, "I'm going up to the island for the weekend," or whatever.

Looking now, I could see there were about ten or twelve cottages, all painted a leaf green with white trim. I asked, "Which one is the Randolph house?"

"It's all the Randolph house." Luke gave me a quick look. "Don't you know the arrangement?"

"What arrangement?"

"Well, you see, each room is a house all to itself, and no two of them are connected."

I stared at him, then at the group of houses that were drawing nearer as the boat glided toward them. "I don't understand," I said.

"Nobody does. It was Mrs. Randolph's idea, hers and her sister's. You see, the living room is one house, the kitchen is another, the dining room is another and each bedroom is a house all to itself. And no two of them are connected."

"I don't believe it. You're putting me on."

"No, I'm not. But you will see for yourself."

"It sounds fantastic."

"It is." He guided the launch into the only vacant place of the four-berth boathouse; then, after getting out, he helped me, saying, "I'll take you to the living room,

11

where you will find Miss Westmore waiting for you; then I'll take your bags over to your bedroom. One of the maids will unpack for you."

I stepped up onto the floor of the boat-house with his help, then stopped and faced him. "You mean Vivienne Westmore is here? Now?"

"I'm afraid so. She and a friend."

"But Mr. Randolph didn't tell me she was going to be here."

"I guess he didn't know. Or he didn't think it would make any difference."

I stopped myself from saying, "Well, it does!"

But to know why it made any difference to me, it would be necessary to go back a year and a half to the time when I first went to work as private secretary to Douglas Randolph, President of Amalgamated Fabrics, Inc.

I was all of nineteen, fresh out of secretarial school after completing two years at Greenbrier College, and very thrilled to get such a good job right away and at such a marvelous salary.

I'll never forget the day I went to apply for the job. I was scared stiff.

The offices of Amalgamated Fabrics were

as impressive as its president. They were on one of the top floors of the Pan Am Building that towers over Grand Central Station and had paneled walls and soft luscious carpets. To get to the office of the president you first went into a reception room that could have doubled for a movie set. In the center of the room was a large, flat-topped desk at which sat an imposing blonde of ample proportions. There were four phones on the desk, and she managed to talk into all of them at the same time in a voice sweet enough to put honey to shame.

When I approached the desk, with my knees trembling, she smiled at me, hung up one phone and asked, "May I help you?"

I said, "I hope so. I'm Miss Foster from the Chandler Secretarial School. I have an appointment with Mr. Randolph at eleven."

Her smile broadened, showing a perfect set of teeth and a dimple in each cheek. "Oh yes," she said. "You came about the job as Mr. Randolph's secretary."

I said, "Yes, I did."

The unused phone rang, and as she picked it up she said to me, "Just have a seat, and I'll notify Mr. Randolph's secretary you are here."

I looked around the large, beautifully furnished room, which was occupied by men and women of various ages who I presumed were buyers. There was one high-backed armchair vacant, and I went over to it and sank down upon its dark red brocade seat. Apprehension began to fill me. I was sure a man who was president of a place like this would want a more dashing secretary than I: little Karen Foster of Rye, New York, who was still living at home with her mother and kid brother.

I hadn't heard the receptionist announce me because she spoke into the phones in a voice so low she could not be heard even a few feet away, so I was surprised when a middle-aged woman, beautifully groomed and wearing a navy blue tailored dress, came into the room from a hallway and walked directly over to me. "Miss Foster?" she asked. She didn't smile, but her voice and manner were kindly.

I stood up and said, "Yes."

"Come this way, please," the woman said, crossing the room toward the hallway. As we walked along together, she went on, "I'm Mrs. Matthews. I've been Mr. Randolph's secretary for five years, ever since the beginning of Amalgamated Fabrics, but now my husband wants me to give up my job and stay home."

I said, "Oh?"

She said, "You'll like working for Mr. Randolph. He's a very exceptional man, and you are just the kind of a girl he wants."

I laughed nervously. "Oh, but he hasn't even seen me," I protested.

She smiled then. "Don't worry about it," she told me. "I know him so well, I can tell."

We had been walking along the hallway, which had private offices on each side. Eventually we came to a corner room with a dark paneled door on which was printed in gold: "Douglas Randolph, President."

Mrs. Matthews opened the door and ushered me into a large, pine-paneled room with a soft beige wall-to-wall carpet, comfortable upholstered leather chairs and a sofa of brown. One wall was covered with bookshelves, the other three walls with paintings that looked like originals. There was even a fireplace, but it being late spring, there was no fire burning.

There was a corner formed by large floor-to-ceiling windows draped with beige silk at the sides. Before these was a large glass-topped walnut desk, and in a high-backed, carved walnut armchair was sitting the handsomest man I had ever seen. He looked about thirty-two or three. As Mrs. Matthews and I entered the room, he stood up, came around the desk and over to me.

He was smiling, and he had his hand out-stretched. Mrs. Matthews said, "This is Karen Foster. Karen, Mr. Randolph."

We shook hands, and he said, "Let's sit over here," indicating two chairs from which we could see the entire lower part of the city with its tall, many-windowed towers.

Mrs. Matthews went into a room that opened from one side of the fireplace. I could see it was a small office with a stenographer's desk, a long table and some bookshelves. There was one window that faced north on Park Avenue. Then she closed the door.

Mr. Randolph asked, "When can you start to work?"

I gasped. "But you don't know anything about me. I thought you'd ask me some questions."

He smiled, and I felt suddenly warm and tingly all over. "I know all about you," he told me. "You graduated from secretarial school with high honors. You're a good stenographer, intelligent. You graduated from Greenbrier College at the top of your class, majoring in English Lit. The secretarial school had all the statistics. In addition to that, you are most attractive and exactly what I need here."

I couldn't believe my ears, so I'm afraid I just sat and stared. He was, without doubt, the best-looking man I have even seen or ever dared dream of. He was tall, broad-shouldered, with slender hips. His hair was chestnut brown, and he wore it cut short and brushed back from a side part. The new generation might say he wore it in an old-fashioned style, but on him everything looked as up-to-date as tomorrow's news. His eyes were large and brown with a twinkle in them. His forehead was high, and his nose straight. He had a large mouth with nicely shaped lips that could either be firm or stretch into a smile that would melt a heart of stone. And my heart was not made of stone, and at that particular moment it was free of entanglements, which, of course, left it vulnerable. He had a square chin with a cleft in it that seemed to deepen when he concentrated on something and tightened the corners of his mouth. He was concentrating on my astonished face at that moment, and after a while he began to chuckle. He asked, "Would a salary of a hundred and twenty-five dollars a week be all right?"

At that I opened my mouth, but no sound came out. The school had told me maybe eighty-five dollars to start. When I didn't say anything, he suggested, "Maybe you'd like to go home and think about it and talk it over with your mother."

I managed to find my voice and asked, "How did you know I have a mother?"

He grinned. "Any girl as naïve as you in this day and age must have a mother."

I blushed then and realized I must be acting like a perfect fool.

He got up, turned to his desk and touched a button. Instantly the door to Mrs. Matthews' office opened and she came toward me, smiling. "Everything all settled?" she asked.

Mr. Randolph said, "As far as I am concerned, it is. Maybe you can get an answer from Miss Foster on the way to the reception room."

She took my arm and asked him, "What did you do — scare her to death?"

He laughed. "Apparently. But maybe if you vouch for me and assure her I'm harmless, you can persuade her to come in Monday, so you can begin showing her the ropes."

"Okay," she said. "Come on, Miss Foster. The worst is over. After this, there's nothing to it."

I smiled at Mr. Randolph then, beginning to get myself under control. I said, "Thank you, Mr. Randolph. I'll be here Monday. Nine o'clock?"

"Nine-thirty is early enough," he told me, and began looking at some letters on his desk.

On the way back to the reception room, Mrs. Matthews said, "Just one thing. You might as well know it right away. He is very much in love with his wife."

I was glad we had reached the reception room by then, so all I had to say was, "Thank you. I'll see you Monday."

She smiled. "I'm sure you'll like it here. Everybody does."

"I'm sure I shall," I said, and with a wave of goodbye I hurried over to a waiting elevator.

When I got home and told my mother I had the job and what it paid, she wasn't as enthusiastic as I'd expected her to be. "It sounds too good to be true," was her comment.

"That's what I thought at first. But maybe there are lots of jobs just as good all over the city; only we never hear of them."

"I doubt it." My mother stood looking at me for a moment, and I saw worry in her fading blue eyes. "What kind of a man is he?" she asked.

She had a pretty face with small regular

features, soft brown hair touched with gray, and a still slender and very good figure. She hadn't been well lately, and I was glad to be able to take some of the financial burden from her shoulders. My father, who had died three years ago, had been an advertising man, and although he had been a successful one, he hadn't left too much money and my mother had been having to pinch pennies to keep me and my brother in school. Now I could make it easier for her.

"Handsome and kind."

She tightened her lips. "That's what I was afraid of," she said. "Is he married?"

I laughed. "Of course. Isn't every boss?" I didn't mention Mrs. Matthews' remark about how much in love with his wife he was.

My mother sighed. "Well, just watch your step," she said. "Falling in love with a married man only ends in heartbreak for somebody — usually the girl."

"Oh, Mother!" I cried. "I'm not going to fall in love with him!"

My first day on the job, he was out of the office, and Mrs. Matthews said she was glad, because it would give her more time to break me in. "One of the most important parts of the job," she told me, "is to protect him from people he doesn't want to see."

"But how will I know who these people are?"

"You'll learn. Some of them are family. Particularly his wife."

"But I thought he was so much in love with his wife."

She slammed a desk drawer shut. "Oh, I don't mean that he isn't always glad to see her. He's crazy about her. But sometimes she doesn't understand that during the day he has business to transact and can't go out for long, leisurely lunches, unless they are business dates. *His* business."

I didn't get the significance of that remark for quite a few days. I said, "I see." But I really didn't.

There was a picture of Mrs. Randolph on his desk in a tooled leather frame, and I picked it up and looked at it. "She's lovely," I said. And she was: a very pretty face with a tantalizing smile, nice blonde hair and eyes that must be blue. Judging from as much of her figure as the portrait picture showed, the figure was worthy of the face.

"Yes, she is lovely," Mrs. Matthews agreed. "And she's as nice as she looks. But — well, she is inclined to be possessive, if you know what I mean."

"Yes, I know. But that is probably because she loves him."

21

"Yes, she does. Very much. And he loves her."

The picture was signed:

"All my love
          "Ariadne"

"Ariadne," I said aloud. "It's a pretty name. I never heard it but once before. There is a pianist by that name. Ariadne Westmore. They pronounce it Ar-ee-ad-nee."

"That's she," Mrs. Matthews said.

I replaced the photograph. "Really?" I said. "How interesting. I love her playing. I have all her records, and I always try to go to her concerts. She specializes in Chopin, who is my favorite."

"That's right," Mrs. Matthews said. "She's very good. And that's another thing. Her manager, Rudolph Vanderhoff, is another one Mr. Randolph likes to avoid whenever possible."

This surprised me. "Oh? Why?"

"Because he wants to exploit Ariadne, book her around the world. And Mr. Randolph won't allow it."

"Oh? Does she want to go?"

"Yes and no. She'd like the publicity, but she wouldn't want to be away from her husband that long."

"I can understand that." Then I asked, "I suppose Westmore is her maiden name?"

"That's right. She's something of a women's lib person, so she uses her maiden name professionally."

I said, "I see. Anyone else I ought to know about?"

"Just her sister, Vivienne. But she doesn't come into the office very often."

"Is she nice?" It was a natural question, and I was surprised when Mrs. Matthews answered me by just one word, "Putrid!"

I had to laugh. "At least you're graphic." She smiled ruefully. "You'll find out. She's Ariadne's twin sister, but not pretty and sweet the way Ariadne is." Then she elaborated, "It seems they were very close when they were growing up; then when Ariadne began to show an aptitude for the piano and went to Juilliard to study seriously, they began to drift apart. Vivienne tried to sing, but didn't have a good enough voice to be taken seriously, so she finally gave it up. Their parents died when they were in their late teens, leaving them rather comfortably off, and they took a large, old-fashioned apartment in the Chelsea section of the city. Vivienne didn't like the idea of Ariadne getting married and leaving her alone, but she kept the apartment. Ariadne tried to keep in touch with her, including her in their social life, but Vivienne just didn't fit in. So they began to drift farther and farther apart, and Vivienne began to get interested in different cults and to take them too seriously. She was always going to meetings and things like that. She's practically rude to Mr. Randolph, but I think that is because she kind of likes him herself."

"That's too bad," I said. "But maybe she'll get married herself some day."

"I doubt it, unless she marries some queer like herself."

I didn't know what to say to that, so I kept still. Eventually Mrs. Matthews said, "Well, I guess that's all in the personal line, except for Jason."

"Who is he?"

"Jason is the chauffeur and very devoted to both of them. You'll meet him eventually, and any time you need anything you can always count on him."

The phone rang, and she answered it, saying, "No, he won't be in today. He had to go over to the New Jersey factory." When she hung up, she explained, "We have several factories: one in Paterson, one in Hartford, one in Chicago, one in Salem, South Carolina and one in Montreal. You'll get to know the various managers and the salesmen. It will take time, but everybody is very nice. Oh, and you'll have to familiarize yourself with the various fabrics and the prices of them, both wholesale and retail."

I guess I looked frightened, because she smiled and said, "It sounds formidable, but it will become second nature to you after a while."

"I'm sure it will."

She went to a shelf and came back with a large book made of large squares of material instead of pages. In the upper right-hand corner of each piece of material was pasted a label on which was written the contents of the material and its width and price, both wholesale and retail. "You take a look at this while I take a look at the mail," she said.

I said, "Okay," and sat down at a long table at the side of her office where she deposited the sample book. Then, as she began opening and sorting the mail, she said, "Oh yes, one more thing. Look out for Alicia."

I asked, "Who is Alicia?"

"Alicia Kierny, the receptionist. She'd eat the boss with salt and pepper if she got the chance."

"And I'm supposed not to give her the chance?"

"That's the general idea."

★ ★ ★

The first time I met Ariadne, I was pleasantly surprised. She was even prettier and more gracious close to than she was on the stage.

I was alone in my office, which opened off Mr. Randolph's, when she came in. It was the first week I'd been on my own. Mrs. Matthews had left the previous Friday, and fortunately for me, Mr. Randolph was out of the office a lot, so I was able to get used to things gradually.

I heard the door to Mr. Randolph's office open and got up to see who it was. It was Mrs. Randolph. She was wearing a light blue dress that matched her eyes and a wisp of veil on her beautifully coiffed blonde hair. I said, "Oh! I thought I heard someone come in."

She smiled and said, "Good morning. I'm Ariadne Westmore, and you must be Karen Foster."

I said, "Yes, I am. How do you do, Mrs. Randolph."

She came to me and held out her hand. "I'm so glad to meet you, Karen," she said. "My husband mentioned he had a new secretary, but he didn't tell me how pretty you are."

I guess I blushed and said awkwardly, "Thank you."

26

"Is he in?" she asked.

I said, "No. He went up to the Hartford factory today."

She frowned slightly. "Oh dear! I wish he'd told me. I wanted to have lunch with him."

"I'm sure he'll be sorry he missed you."

She shrugged. "Well, I'll just call my manager and have lunch with him instead." She went to Mr. Randolph's desk and dialed a number. When someone answered, she said, "Rudy, take me to lunch?"

Whatever he responded made her laugh. Then she said, "I'll be at Twenty-One in half an hour. Call Louis and reserve our regular table." She hung up and turned to me. "By the way, do you like music?"

"Oh yes," I said, deciding she wouldn't be interested in the fact that I'd studied piano for six years.

She opened a blue straw purse, took out two tickets and gave them to me. "I'm giving a concert at Town Hall next Wednesday. Please come."

I took the tickets. "Thank you. I'll be very glad to. As a matter of fact, I always go to your concerts. I went even before I knew who you were."

She raised her beautifully shaped eyebrow. "Before you knew who I was? I don't understand."

27

"I mean, before I came to work here and discovered you were Mrs. Randolph."

She hesitated a moment, then said, "Yes, you are right. I *am* Mrs. Randolph, Mrs. Douglas Randolph, wife of the president of Amalgamated Fabrics, Inc. I am also Ariadne Westmore." She smiled sweetly at me as she closed her purse. "And I play the piano."

I felt rebuked, but before I could think of something diplomatic to say, she turned and walked out, closing the door after her.

In a couple of minutes the phone rang, and when I answered it it was Alicia. She asked, "And what did her majesty want today?"

I had to think quickly. "Oh, she just stopped in to leave a message for Mr. Randolph."

"I suppose it's private?"

"Oh yes," I said sweetly. "Has the coffee wagon been around yet?"

"It's on its way," Alicia said. "Bye now."

When I'd replaced the receiver, I sat looking at it for a moment, thinking to myself, I'm beginning to understand some of the things Mrs. Matthews told me that first day.

Chapter Two

The next morning Mr. Randolph said, "My wife tells me she stopped in yesterday."

I said, "Yes. And she was kind enough to give me two tickets to her concert next Wednesday."

He said, "Oh? Are you going?"

"Oh, yes. As a matter of fact, I always go to her concerts. I play the piano a little myself, and I am quite a fan of hers."

He looked out the window thoughtfully, and although it wasn't a clear enough day to see very far downtown, I had the feeling he wouldn't have seen any of it even if it had been visible. His look was more inward than outward. After a moment he said, "She's a very fine artist."

I said, "Yes, she is. You must be very proud of her."

"Yes, I am," he said. Then, changing the subject abruptly, he asked, "Can you take some letters?"

I said, "Of course," and got my stenographer's book and my pen.

He dictated for nearly an hour, and I found I had no difficulty keeping up with him. As he dictated he seldom looked at me, but for the most part looked over the top of my head.

At one time the phone rang, and I answered it for him. A man's voice said, "Mr. Randolph, please. Tell him it's Rudy Vanderhoff."

I told him, holding out the phone so he could reach it. The corners of his mouth tightened and the cleft in his chin deepened as he took the phone. "Yes, Rudy?" he said. Then he listened for a few moments, staring up at the ceiling. I couldn't hear what the man was saying, but I couldn't help but hear Mr. Randolph's response. It was: "Definitely not! I don't care how much money she'd make. She doesn't need any more money, and I won't have her traveling all over the world without me."

The manager said something else, and Mr. Randolph answered, "No, I won't have lunch with you. There is nothing more for us to talk about. Ariadne knows exactly how I feel about the whole thing." Then he hung up the phone with a bang. He didn't start dictating immediately, and I didn't know whether to wait or get up and go into my own office. After a few minutes' silence, he asked, "Now, where were we?"

I said, "You were dictating a letter to a

George Swanson at the Salem factory about a new machine." He said, "Oh, yes," and began to dictate where he'd left off. But when he finished that letter he said, "That will be all for now." So I closed my book, got up and went into my office. I was sorry I had had to listen to that phone conversation. I didn't want to know anything about my boss's personal life. But it was my first experience as a secretary, and I supposed things such as that phone conversation were unavoidable.

When Mr. Randolph went out to lunch, he said, "I won't be back. If anybody wants me, I'll be in all day tomorrow."

I asked, "What about those letters? Won't you be back to sign them?"

He said, "No. You sign them for me."

The afternoon went along smoothly enough until about four o'clock, when Alicia phoned in and said, "Mr. Vanderhoff is here."

I said, "Oh! Tell him Mr. Randolph is out and won't be back."

I heard her repeat my message; then she said, "He says he wants to see you."

A feeling of impending disaster crept into the pit of my stomach. "But I don't want to see him!" I said.

She laughed softly. "He's already halfway

there," she told me. And just as I replaced the receiver, the door opened and a rather nice-looking man came in. He was tall and well built; blond, with hair just a trifle too long, sideburns and heavy eyebrows. He had on an English-type suit with high-cut lapels and a scarf around his neck instead of a tie. He smiled, and most girls would have reacted favorably to it, but instinctively I distrusted him. "Hi," he said. "I'm Rudy Vanderhoff, Ariadne's manager."

I said, "Oh?"

He said, "I thought it would be a good idea if you and I got acquainted."

I looked him right in the eyes and was shocked to see they were black and shiny, like old-fashioned shoe buttons — a sharp contrast to his blond hair. I said, "I don't really see any reason for it."

He seemed surprised at that but recovered quickly and smiled. His teeth were large and not too even. "But of course," he said. "We can be a great deal of help to each other."

"I don't see how."

He had a large box of candy under one arm. He gave it to me. "Maybe this will sweeten you up a bit," he said.

I put the box on the desk. "What is it you want, Mr. Vanderhoff?" I asked.

He kept his smile and his cool. "Nothing at the moment," he assured me. "But one of these days I'd like to buy you a lunch or a cocktail."

"That's very kind of you," I told him. "But no, thank you."

He stopped smiling then, and I was afraid I'd been too abrupt. I said, "I'm sorry, Mr. Vanderhoff, and thank you for the candy, but I have a rather full personal life outside the office." This was anything but true, but it was the first thing I could think of to say.

He nodded. "I understand." He gave me a penetrating look, and I had the feeling he could see right through my clothing. "A beautiful girl like you would have." He walked toward the door; then he turned back to me. "No need to tell Mr. Randolph I was here," he said. He hesitated. Then he smiled, and I couldn't resist asking, "Nor Mrs. Randolph?"

He kept the smile intact and raised rather heavy eyebrows. "As a matter of fact, it was her idea," he told me, and went out and closed the door.

After he'd gone, I stood looking at the box of candy. I didn't want it, yet I didn't believe in wasting anything. Finally I took it out to the girls in the typing room. "Compliments of a customer," I told them. They were delighted. Anything for a break in the monotony of typing hour after hour.

I didn't know whether or not to mention Rudy's visit to Mr. Randolph. I decided against it. If Mrs. Randolph wanted to tell him, that was up to her. Apparently she didn't, because nothing was ever said to me about it.

The day of Ariadne's concert, my mother and I planned to have dinner in town. She would come in and meet me at five, and we would dine at a little restaurant in the fifties that was authentically French and very reasonable. Dickie, my brother, was seventeen, a senior in high school, and had so many friends he was always able to take care of himself if my mother and I went out.

When I bade good night to Mr. Randolph, I said, "I suppose I'll see you at the concert this evening."

He looked at me in surprise. "Oh, no. No, I'm afraid not. You see, I never go to my wife's concerts."

I was taken aback, and I guess I showed my surprise, because he smiled and said, "You see, I found I wasn't needed. And the husband of a performing artist is only in the way standing around backstage. Her manager takes care of everything pertaining to the concert, and then I take

34

them to supper afterwards."

I don't know why I should have felt embarrassed, but I did. I said, "Oh. Well, good night."

He said, "Good night. I hope you enjoy the concert."

I said, "I'm sure I shall."

Later, as my mother and I sat in the auditorium waiting for the curtains to part and Ariadne to come out onto the stage, I began to wonder if Vivienne was there anywhere. We had very good seats, quite far front and center, and I glanced around to see if there was any woman there who could possibly be Ariadne's sister. I saw no one who resembled her and decided perhaps she was backstage, maybe in the dressing room with her sister.

When finally the curtains parted, the lights dimmed, the spot was thrown on the stage and Ariadne walked out, I found I was holding my breath. She was exquisite. She had on a pale blue floor-length gown, Empire style, with a low-cut neck and sleeveless, and her arms were beautiful. So was her figure. My mother and I joined in the welcoming applause, and she accepted the tribute with a faint smile and a momentarily bowed head. Then she sat down at the concert grand piano, and the audience was immediately hushed and expectant.

It was a memorable evening and one I would never forget. The program was entirely Chopin, with Schumann encores. At the end the audience gave her a standing ovation and many curtain calls and begged for as many encores as she would play. Tears of emotion came to my eyes, and I wondered how any man could not love her. She was everything that was beautiful, desirable and feminine, and had that wonderful talent thrown in. It was difficult for me to understand how her husband could stay away from her concert. Even if he wasn't musical, and I didn't know whether or not he was, I should have thought he would have wanted to be there to share her triumph with her. But he had said he met them later and took them to supper. Who was *them?* Ariadne, Rudy and Vivienne?

As the curtains closed on the final encore and curtain call, and the audience quieted down and the lights came on, my mother said, "That was very enjoyable." I looked at her in surprise. She had spoken so matter-of-factly, and I had been so ecstatically transported, almost into another world. Or was I exaggerating to myself? Just because I was becoming attached to my boss, and I had to admit I was, did I also have to be affected by his wife? But surely she had a magnetism that was almost unearthly.

Then, as they say in books, as my mother and I slowly walked up the aisle to the exit I faced a moment of truth. Was I getting too interested in my boss? Had I better look for masculine companionship elsewhere?

I had liked several boys and men while I was in college and had had my share of dates, but there had never been anyone who, as they say, made bells ring. Was my boss, Douglas Randolph, beginning to make me hear those bells? And in so short a time? If so, I'd better give up the job and get something else. There were a couple of young men at the beach club in Rye where we lived with whom I sometimes swam and danced, but I'd never wanted to get to know them more than casually. So maybe I'd better. As my mother would be only too glad to remind me, falling in love with a married man was very unproductive, and someone always got hurt, usually the girl.

The next morning I bought all the papers to see what the music critics had said of the concert. They all were more than complimentary, one going so far as to say, "The pity of it is we are privileged to hear Miss Westmore only once a year, and it isn't enough."

I wondered what her husband would say to that, if anything. But I dared not ask him, and all he said to me about the concert was to ask me politely if my mother and I had enjoyed it.

I said, "Yes! Oh yes! I've never heard her play better."

His lips tightened, and the cleft in his chin deepened. "That's what Rudy told me. And Vivienne." Then he asked, "Have you met Vivienne yet?"

I said, "No. She's your wife's sister, isn't she?"

He said, "Yes. They're twins, but not at all alike."

Inanely I said, "That happens sometimes."

The phone rang, and he answered it himself, saying, "Oh yes, Vivienne." He gave me a little smile as if saying, "Speak of the devil." Then he said into the phone, "What is it you want? A heavy black silk? Twenty yards? Okay, I'll order it for you." Then, "No, I haven't seen the papers. Well, that's nice."

Vivienne seemed to have quite a lot to say, and he listened impatiently for a while, then interrupted her. "Please, Vivienne, I get enough of that from Rudy. I am not being selfish, and I am not depriving the world of the pleasure of hearing my wife play. She's made a lot of records, and they can buy those. Now, if you'll excuse me, I'm busy and have several people out in the reception room waiting for me. Goodbye."

He hung up before she could say anything else and, getting up from his desk, strode out of the room. He didn't tell me where he was going, and I thought he'd be back in a few minutes, because I knew there was no one waiting for him in the reception room. But he didn't come back, and for the rest of the morning I had to make excuses when anyone asked for him, even people in the office. I thought maybe he'd phone me and tell me where he was, but he didn't.

It was that afternoon that I had my first encounter with Vivienne. She came striding into the office without being announced first. Alicia had just time to call me and say, "Batten down the hatches. Vivienne Westmore is on her way in."

I said, "Thank you," and had just replaced the receiver when the door burst open and a rather exotically dressed woman entered. She looked around the office and asked, "Where is my brother-in-law?"

I said, "He had to go out. May I help you? I'm his secretary, Karen Foster."

She looked me over critically. "So you're

the new one, are you?"

I said, "Yes, I guess I am."

She sniffed. "Well, you're an improvement on the old battle-axe he had for so long."

I didn't know whether to smile or not, so I didn't. She was dressed in green, several different shades that swayed like a willow in the wind when she moved. The cut and style of the dress defied analysis, and I wasn't interested enough to bother. I was more interested in the girl who was wearing it. She was very unlike Ariadne in looks. Whereas Ariadne was beautiful, Vivienne was plain. Not homely exactly, but plain. She also had blonde hair and blue eyes, but there was no life to her hair, which she had cut short, and her eyes were expressionless. She asked, "Will my brother-in-law be back soon?"

"I don't believe so. Is there anything I can do for you?"

She looked annoyed. "Did he leave any material for me? I called him this morning about getting me some fabric. Did he?"

I hesitated. "Not as far as I know. That is, not yet."

Her face seemed to change. From the plain, negative expression with the expressionless eyes, her face took on a vicious, evil look. She asked, "Well, didn't he leave me any message or anything?"

I said, "No, he didn't. He had to rush out quite unexpectedly."

"Oh! Sometimes I could throttle him!" She fairly screamed the words at me, as if it were my fault, and her eyes seemed suddenly to flash sparks, piercing sparks, like white darts. It seemed so real that I crazily imagined the darts were piercing my face and neck, like sharp pins. Instinctively I drew back from her, actually frightened, and automatically I fingered a small silver cross which I was wearing on a thin silver chain around my neck. It had been a piece of jewelry my mother had given me when I was a child of five, and I wore it sometimes because I knew it pleased her to have me do so.

In a voice that sounded hollow in my own ears, I said to Vivienne, "I'm very sorry about the fabric. If you will tell me just what it is you want, perhaps I can call the factory over in Jersey and have it delivered by special messenger. Would you like to see the sample book?"

As I was speaking and nervously fingering the tiny silver cross around my neck, she began to back away from me, even as I had backed away from her. The evil expression seemed to melt from her face and the sparks to go out in her eyes, the way a skyrocket, having reached its height, begins to fade away; and she was once again the plain, un-attractive girl with the expressionless eyes who was Ariadne's twin sister. She turned toward the door. "Thank you, no," she said. "I'll call my brother-in-law about it at home this evening."

After she'd gone, Alicia called me. "You still in one piece?" she asked.

I said, "Sure, why wouldn't I be?"

"She's a weird one all right," Alicia said. "I always dread to see her come in."

"Oh, come on, now." I laughed, pre-tending a calmness I was far from feeling. "She's not that bad."

Chapter Three

The next morning I asked Mr. Randolph if his sister-in-law had called him about the fabric.

His brow furrowed. "Yes, she did. Will you please call the Paterson factory and order it?" He got the sample book, found a heavy black silky fabric and said, "This one." He slammed the book shut. "Have it delivered here, and I'll have Jason pick it up and take it down to her apartment."

I said, "All right."

Then he asked, "Did you have any trouble with her?"

I didn't know what to say to that, because I couldn't very well tell him about those sparks in her eyes that had seemed to prick me like sharp pins. It would sound crazy and was, of course, just my imagination. So I just said, "Not trouble, actually, but she was quite upset when the material wasn't here."

He said, "Um. I know what you mean." Then he sighed. "Well, if she ever bothers you or tries to give you a hard time, let me know."

43

I said, "Oh, I'm sure she never will." Which showed how naïve I was.

Well, that afternoon I met Jason. He came in to pick up the material that had been rushed by special messenger from the Paterson factory. I was quite impressed by him. He was in a bottle green uniform, with his peaked cap in his hand, and he was a very attractive man. Offhand I guessed him to be about thirty. He was tall and slender, with dark brown hair and eyes. He wasn't exactly good-looking, but there was something likable about his face. He had good teeth and a pleasant smile. He said, "I'm Jason, the chauffeur. I'm supposed to pick up a package for Miss Vivienne."

I said, "Yes. It's right over here," indicating where the factory messenger had left it on a side table.

It was a large, bulky package, but he picked it up as if it were nothing. Then he stopped and turned to me. "You are Miss Foster?" he asked.

I said, "Yes. Karen Foster."

He smiled in a friendly way. "I hope you like it here," he said. "The boss and Mrs. Randolph speak very highly of you."

I couldn't help but feel pleased, although I was surprised that either my boss or his wife would discuss me with the chauffeur. I said, "I'm glad to hear it. I'm very happy here." Then I asked, "I hope you don't mind taking that down to Vivienne?"

He settled the cumbersome package on his left hip and continued his trip to the door. "Oh no," he said. "I'm glad to do anything for Miss Vivienne." Then, just before going out, he said, "And anything I can do for you, just let me know."

I said, "Thank you." I could see why Mrs. Matthews would say he was very reliable.

That was in June. Then suddenly, in the early part of July, my world collapsed around my head. My mother died in her sleep one night of what the doctor diagnosed as a massive heart attack, and the week after the funeral, my brother Dickie, who had turned eighteen, was drafted. I was bewildered and don't know what I would have done if it hadn't been for my boss and his wife. They were both wonderful to me. Ariadne helped me find an apartment in the city, because I couldn't stay in the house in Rye all alone, and Jason drove us around from place to place during our apartment search, giving advice about neighborhoods. This one would not be safe for a girl alone; another was too expensive: some were too inaccessible. But at last we found a very pleasant two-room apartment just off Fifth

Avenue on West 12th Street. It was expensive, but Mr. Randolph gave me a raise, saying he wanted me to be happy and not to have to worry about finances. He also helped me sell our house in Rye and advised me to put the money from the sale into what he called blue chip stocks, jointly with Dickie, so I would have an income besides my salary and Dickie would have a nest egg when he came out of the army.

Dickie and I tried to be brave when we said goodbye to each other; and then, all too soon, I was living alone in the Greenwich Village apartment which I'd furnished with the best of the furniture from the house. Special pieces that Dickie thought he'd like to have were put into storage for him. And then he was gone. After a very short training period in the States, suddenly his address was somewhere in Vietnam.

Jason had been very sweet about helping me move, taking the most valuable and breakable articles in the limousine at off times when the Randolphs didn't need him or the car. During our rides back and forth, he never presumed to be friendly or familiar, but always kept his place as the chauffeur and treated me as if I were a member of the Randolph family instead of just the secretary.

For several nights, while my apartment was being painted, I was invited to stay with the Randolphs at their East 79th Street house, and during that time they were very tactful about making me feel at home and not like company. Their housekeeper, Mrs. Watson, was also very nice to me. One evening Doug — he had suggested I call him Doug — had to go out to a business dinner, and Ariadne and I had a very pleasant meal alone, talking about music. After dinner Rudy came in. He seemed to be surprised to see me, and I had to admit I was surprised to see him. Ariadne said, "You know Miss Foster, don't you?" and he said, "Yes, we've met."

I let it go at that and said, "Good evening, Mr. Vanderhoff."

We gave each other a casual nod of greeting; then he turned back to Ariadne. "I thought you'd be alone," he said, and it was very evident he was disappointed. "You should have told me when you called me this afternoon."

She gave me a quick sideways glance with her large blue eyes, which I was learning were sometimes glittery rather than pleasant, and to Rudy she gave a surreptitious shake of her head. "Karen is staying with us while her apartment is being painted," she explained, to which he just grunted.

He went over to the ebony concert grand piano at the side of the black and white room and looked over some music that was on the rack. "Come play for me," he said to Ariadne, "I don't get much chance to hear you — alone."

She went over to the piano and sat down on the chair, which she used instead of a bench, and let her fingers wander over the keys. He stood behind her with his hands on her shoulders in what seemed to me an overly familiar manner. I was quite sure he wouldn't have been that familiar if Doug had been there. As a matter of fact, I was sure he wouldn't have been there at all if Doug had been home.

I would have liked to stay and listen to Ariadne play, but I knew they didn't want me, so I said, "If you will excuse me, I have some letters to write," and left the room. If they heard me or even noticed me leave, they gave no indication, and I went up the stairs to my room on the third floor with a heavy heart. But it was none of my business, so I tried to forget it.

When I got up to my room, I threw myself on the bed and listened to the sound of the piano. I could only hear it faintly, but I could tell Ariadne was putting her whole heart into it. She never played in the evenings when Doug was home, and I thought it was strange. But I was gradually learning there were many strange things in their relationship, one of them being that they had separate bedrooms; she had the front room on the second floor, and he had the back one, with a bathroom in between. The house was beautifully furnished, and there was their own private garage in the basement, but somehow it wasn't homelike.

I was glad when a couple of days later, my apartment was ready and I could move into it. I was also glad that Ariadne did not ask me not to mention Rudy's visit to Doug. Of course I didn't, anyway. Nor did Doug ever mention the evening he had gone out during my stay with them.

Doug had given me a week off at the time of my mother's death, and when I returned to the office I had managed to get through the days somehow. Doug hadn't pressed me with too much work, although he managed to keep me busy enough so I wouldn't have time to think. He was very thoughtful that way.

One Friday morning he said, "My wife and I are going up to the lake for the weekend. Jason is picking us up right after lunch."

"The lake?" I couldn't help asking. It was the first time I'd heard of it.

He smiled. "Yes. Lake Tranquil in upper New York State. We have a summer place there. As a matter of fact, we have an island all to ourselves."

"Sounds marvelous," I said.

"It is. You'll have to come up sometime. I'm sure you'd like it." And that was all that was said about it at the time.

Losing my mother and brother so suddenly and so close together had dimmed the sounds of the bells when I was with Doug. He was always very nice to me, but he kept our relationship impersonal at all times, so I gradually began to get over what might have been called my crush on him. The boys I knew in Rye called me occasionally and took me to dinner, but there was nothing serious about our dates, and the summer dragged along, as summers do in a city.

Then in August, tragedy struck the Randolph family. Ariadne disappeared.

One afternoon Doug left the office early, saying, "My wife and I are going out to dinner and the theater with some friends. We're having cocktails at our place first, so I promised I'd get home early and dress in time to receive our guests."

I said, "Well, have a nice time."

He smiled. "Oh, I will. We always enjoy getting together with friends."

I left a little early myself, as there was a movie on Eighth Street I wanted to see. I had dinner and went to the early show, because in view of the way things were in the city of late, I don't like to be out alone after dark.

I'd just gotten home after the movie, about nine-fifteen, when my phone started ringing. Answering it, I found it was Doug. He sounded upset. He said, "Karen, have you heard from Ariadne?"

I said, "Why, no. I thought you and she had a date with friends this evening."

"We did. But when I got home she wasn't here, and Mrs. Watson said she didn't know where she was."

"Have you called Vivienne and Rudy?"

"Yes, of course. Neither of them is home. But then they never are."

"Have you called the police?"

"No! I don't want to bring them into it."

"Maybe Rudy got a sudden engagement for her to play somewhere?"

"Even so, she'd at least have left me a note or told Mrs. Watson."

"Yes, I suppose she would." Then I asked, "What does Mrs. Watson say?"

"She said Ariadne got a phone call shortly

after breakfast and dressed and went out, saying she'd probably be back for lunch but not to bother fixing anything special."

"And she didn't come home for lunch?"

"No. And that's the last Mrs. Watson had seen or heard of her."

"Oh dear!" was all I could think of to say.

He heaved a deep sigh. "Well, sorry to bother you. She'll probably turn up."

I said, "Yes, I'm sure she will," thinking, perhaps unfairly, She's probably with Rudy somewhere. But she hadn't turned up by the next day. And when Doug finally got in touch with Vivienne and Rudy, and both of them said they hadn't seen or heard from Ariadne the previous day or evening, he decided to call the police. And of course the police immediately began questioning everybody, including me.

Doug didn't come into the office for several days, and when he did he looked awful. I had all I could do to keep from putting my arms around his neck and trying to comfort him, but of course I couldn't do anything like that.

He sat down in his desk chair and put his face in his hands, and for a few minutes neither of us said anything. Then he looked up at me as I stood helplessly beside his desk and asked, "What am I going to do, Karen?"

I sat down in a chair that was on the opposite side of the desk. "Do you want to talk about it, or would you rather not?" I asked him.

He stared at me for a moment, and I could tell he wasn't seeing me at all. Then he began to talk. "I can't understand it," he said. "That morning everything was perfectly all right when I left for work. She was sitting at the breakfast table reading her mail. She had on some kind of a soft blue robe trimmed with lace and —" he sighed and rubbed his white face vigorously with his hands before completing the sentence — "she looked beautiful." He sighed again. "Well, I kissed her goodbye and said I'd be home early enough to dress and have cocktails mixed by the time our friends arrived. And then, as usual, I left.

"When I went out of the house, Jason was waiting for me in the limousine, as usual, and he had put *The New York Times* on the back seat for me, as usual. He always gets it for me every morning. So, to make a long story short, I got into the car, said, 'Good morning, Jason,' picked up the paper and began to scan the news. But you know — it was the strangest thing — my wife's face seemed to come between me and the printed page. I shook the paper to dispel the vision, but as soon as the paper became steady again, Ariadne's face returned. What was it? I wondered. Was there something her eyes were trying to tell me? But if there had been anything she'd wanted to tell me, she would have done it at breakfast. She never kept anything from me, as far as I know. We've always been very close and confided in each other about everything." At this point I had a hard time keeping still, but I managed to, and he went on, "The only arguments we ever have are caused by Rudy urging her to give more concerts and go on the road. Yet as I thought of it, while the car was racing down Second Avenue, I wondered if there hadn't been something in Ariadne's eyes that morning that were appealing to me for help. Was it fear I had seen there? But of course not. That was ridiculous. She had nothing to fear. We have financial security, and we're both perfectly healthy, thank God.

"To be sure, as president of Amalgamated Fabrics, I'm not able to give her as much time as I'd like to, but she is very understanding about that and keeps herself occupied with her charities and her music. And she has Vivienne and lots of friends."

Getting him back to the line of his story, I asked, "And that is all she said to Mrs. Watson?"

He said, "Yes. But after the phone call she dressed hastily in a blue linen suit, walking shoes, and took a shoulder-strap blue leather purse with her."

"And no one in the neighborhood saw her go out or noticed in which direction she went when she left the house?"

"No. She has her own car; a small white convertible with a black top. But she left it in the garage, which is, as you know, under the house. And Jason wasn't back from bringing me down to the office when she left, so he didn't see her. If she was picked up by a friend, no one noticed, and all of her friends claim not to have heard from her or to have communicated with her that day. When the alarm was given out to the police that she was missing, no taxi driver remembered picking up a woman of her description on that day. Airlines, trains, boats and every exit from the city were checked. No one had seen a pretty blonde woman of her description."

As a matter of fact, he didn't tell me any more than he had already told the police, and it had been in all the papers and on the radio and TV news. But I knew it helped him to talk about it, so I listened as if it were all new to me.

Then other things began happening in the

world and the press, and the police lost interest. But not those intimately connected with the affair. For instance, Vivienne made it her business to keep Ariadne's memory fresh in Doug's mind by constantly talking about her. She spent considerable time at the 79th Street house under the pretense of keeping Doug from being lonely, but I could see her presence annoyed him and that he didn't like her.

As usual in such cases, rumors came from all over the world that Ariadne had been seen in various places, but when they were tracked down there was no truth in them. Naturally, I couldn't help but wonder if Rudy had smuggled her out of the country for a concert tour. But if this had been the case, he would have gone with her, and she would eventually have turned up in some part of the world, giving a concert. But Rudy seemed as heartbroken about her mysterious disappearance as was her husband, and it appeared as if he loved her as much as Doug did.

At first he kept in close touch with Doug, but after a few months he began to drift away. He got himself a new client to manage, a man violinist, and he was able to take him on world tours, so that seemed to be that.

Doug threw himself into his business, and as far as I knew had no social life at all. He was trying to buy a factory in England to manufacture tweeds, and that kept him traveling back and forth to Britain frequently.

When he was in the office, he talked to me more than he used to, telling me about his trips and asking my advice about after-dinner speeches he sometimes had to make at evening business meetings. But there was never anything personal about our relationship. I noticed a few gray hairs appearing at the sides of his head above his ears, but I never mentioned them. We were just good pals, although I began to hear those distant bells ringing again sometimes when we were together for any length of time. He was one sweet guy. I tried making new men friends, but it didn't help, and I guess I didn't make any more impression on them than they did on me, because they never lasted very long.

Then, to my surprise, one day in the office Doug said to me, "Make out a check to Jason for six months' salary in lieu of notice. He's leaving."

I guess I gasped, because Doug frowned. "I find I don't need him any more."

When Jason came into the office to pick

up the check, Doug was out. I couldn't help saying, "I'm sorry, Jason. I'll miss you."

He wasn't in his usual uniform; instead, he had on a dark business suit, not of the latest cut, but clean and neat. He tried to smile, but it was a dismal failure. "I feel badly about going," he said. "But times change, and we have to roll with the punches. And now, with Mrs. Randolph gone —"

I said, "Yes, I suppose so." I waited for him to say more, but he didn't. He just put the envelope with the check into his coat pocket, bowed and said, "I've enjoyed knowing you, Miss Foster. Goodbye." And before I could answer him, he was gone.

About a week later, Doug said to me, "Oh, by the way, I have a new chauffeur. I find I need someone after all."

I said, "Oh?"

He said, "Yes. His name is Luke, and he comes highly recommended."

I didn't comment on that, and Luke never came into the office the way Jason used to. The first time I met him was one stormy night in November. Doug was going to a business dinner at the Waldorf Astoria Hotel, where he was to make a speech with which I had helped him. Luke was meeting him with the car at the Lexington Avenue entrance to the Grand Central Terminal that goes out through the Graybar Building. And of course our building had an entrance into the station so you could walk through. Doug had changed into a tuxedo in his private men's room in the office, and he looked wonderful, I thought. Looking out of the window, against which a mixture of rain, sleet and snow was beating, he said, "You'd better let me drive you home tonight. It looks pretty bad out there."

I said, "Oh, I don't have far to walk from the bus. I'll be all right. But thanks just the same."

"Even so, you may have trouble getting on a bus, and taxis are always nonexistent in this kind of weather."

So I capitulated and said, "Well, if it won't be too much out of your way. You know I live down on 12th Street, and you are going uptown."

He smiled. "Big deal. Get your things on. Luke can't park more than half a minute on Lexington Avenue, so I have to be there as he comes along."

Luke was just arriving as we ran out of the station door, and we were able to get into the car without getting too wet. When we were settled on the back seat and Doug had given Luke my address, he said, "By the way, Luke, this is Karen Foster, my secretary. Karen, Luke."

Luke and I exchanged greetings, and as the limousine wove in and out of the heavy rush-hour traffic, I tried to get a better look at him. He was older than Jason and heavier. Not good-looking exactly, but attractive in a stern sort of way. He said, "The traffic is pretty bad tonight." And Doug said, "Yes, it always is on a night like this."

I said, "I hope you don't mind going out of your way to take me home, Luke."

He said, "Not at all." And I liked the caliber of his voice. It was deep and resonant, and he wasn't the least bit subservient, the way Jason used to be sometimes.

When we reached the reconverted red brick house where I had the second floor through, Luke stopped the car, jumped out and came around to open the door for me. And lo and behold! he had a large umbrella to hold over my head as he took my arm and helped me up the front steps to the front door.

As I said good night to Doug I added, "Thanks a lot. And good luck with your speech."

He smiled and nodded. "Thanks to your help, I'm sure it will be a success."

At my front door, I said to Luke, "Thanks again."

He bowed, touched his peaked uniform cap in a salute and said, "It was a pleasure, Miss Foster. I'm glad we had a chance to meet at last."

I said, "Yes. And I'll be seeing you again."

"I hope so."

But we didn't meet again until the office Christmas party, which was held in the ballroom at the Waldorf Astoria. They pulled out all the stops for it and had one of the top dance bands. Everybody was dressed up. Not in evening clothes, because it started at lunch time, with an elaborate buffet lunch which was replenished as needed all during the afternoon. But everybody managed to look his best. I hadn't expected to see Luke there, but why not? He was wearing a dark business suit and could easily have been mistaken for one of the top executives. Seeing me, he came over and asked, "Dance?"

What could I say but, "Love to"?

We danced for a while without talking, as the band was pretty loud. Then between dances Luke asked, "Is the boss here yet? He told me to come on ahead, and he'd take a taxi."

I looked around. Up to that time I hadn't seen Doug, and he hadn't mentioned whether or not he was coming. I had rather doubted it, because up to that time no word had been heard from or about Ariadne. I said, "I don't know. I haven't seen him. I doubt if he'll come this year."

Luke looked serious. "Oh, he'll come all right. He feels he owes it to the company to make an appearance."

"Why?"

Luke shrugged. "He believes the executives should be friendly with all the employees."

"How do you know?"

Luke smiled at that. "We ride around a lot together, and he gets to talking."

"He never says much in the office. That is, he never did until these last few months, but now I guess he gets lonely."

"Yes, I guess so. You are a good person for him to have around."

"How so?"

"Because you are intelligent and know when to listen and when to talk."

I looked at him in surprise. "What makes you think you know so much about me?"

He grinned, and his whole face seemed to light up. "Perhaps I'm a good judge of people."

"You don't seem to be chauffeur material, if I may speak out of turn."

He kept grinning. "Don't you think I'm doing a good job?"

"You must be, or the boss wouldn't keep you." Then, after a moment's silence, I asked, "Do you know why he let Jason go?"

He hesitated, and the grin left his face. "Yes, but I think it's better for you not to know."

I gave him a quick look of surprise. "That's a strange thing to say."

A furrow appeared on his brow. "It's a strange situation."

"It's all of that," I had to agree.

Then I saw Doug coming toward us. He began to smile. "I've been looking for you," he said. "Hello, Luke."

Luke said, "Nice party."

Doug looked around the crowded room. Everyone seemed to be having a good time. "It seems to be." The band began to play again, and Doug asked Luke, "Mind if I steal Miss Foster for a dance?"

Luke bowed and grinned. "You're the boss. How can I object?" So I went into Doug's arms, and we began to dance. To say he was a perfect dancer would be an understatement, and being in his arms, even though it was only on a crowded dance floor, was a large slice of heaven. But I caught hold of myself and talked some silent sense into my silly head before I showed how I felt.

After a few minutes, his arm tightened around me and my heart gave a jump. I hoped he couldn't feel it. "You are as good a dancer as you are a secretary," he told me.

I managed a smile. "And you are as nice a dancer as you are a boss," I countered.

He laughed and held me close. To change the subject, I asked, "Is Vivienne here?"

He sobered immediately. "No. She never comes to these things. She doesn't like to dance. My wife always used to stop in for a while, but never Vivienne."

The mention of his wife put a damper on all the festivities as far as I was concerned, but he went on chatting. "I suppose you have plans for Christmas?"

I said, "No, I haven't. Several of our old friends in Rye have invited me for dinner, but somehow I don't feel like going."

He said, "I know what you mean. I feel the same way." We danced without talking for a few minutes. Then he asked, "I don't suppose you'd want to have Christmas dinner with me?"

I looked up at him in surprise. "Wouldn't people think that strange?" I asked.

He shrugged. "Who would know about it? Besides, we wouldn't be doing anything wrong." He smiled faintly. "I promise not to seduce you."

I felt my face flush. "It isn't that. But you really don't know where your wife is."

He sobered immediately. "That's true. But I'm sure she wouldn't mind — if she's around anywhere and could find out."

I wasn't so sure about that. I asked, "What about Vivienne? Won't she expect you to spend Christmas with her?"

"Probably. But I am not going to." Then he added, "There must be some nice quiet little place in the Village where they have good food and no one would know us."

"Oh, there is. Or — well, I could cook dinner in my apartment, if you'd like that."

"I'd like that very much, but it might give you a guilt complex."

"If dining with you anywhere is going to make me feel guilty, I'd rather not do it."

He was silent for a long time, during which the music stopped and Alicia came up to us. Touching Doug on the arm, she smiled at him and said, "No fair dancing with your secretary all the time. You're making the rest of us jealous."

He flushed slightly, then smiled. "Then may I have the next dance with you?"

She hugged his arm closer to her ample bosom. "That's what I had in mind," she told him with an arch smile.

He winked at me. "Will you excuse me, Miss Foster?"

I couldn't help smiling. "Of course," I said, and turned away.

Instantly Luke was beside me. "Wouldn't you like something to eat?" he asked. "And I'll bet you haven't even had a drink yet."

"It's a little early in the day for that, for me," I told him.

He grinned. "You mean the sun hasn't come over the yardarm yet?"

"It hasn't even come up over Madison Avenue yet."

"Dear, dear!" he said with mock seriousness. Then, "Well, you can at least have some turkey and ham and salad. It will give you a good foundation for later."

"It should." I let him lead me the length of the room to where a long and bountifully laden table was set and being waited on by white-coated waiters. When our plates were full, we found a small empty table to one side where we could eat in comparative seclusion. When we were seated, Luke asked, "Have you become very well acquainted with any of the out-of-town factory people?"

I had to admit I hadn't. Some of them I knew via the phone, but I'd never met any of them face to face.

"Doug — that is, Mr. Randolph — should take you on a tour of the factories sometime."

I said, "Yes, I'd like that."

He said, "I guess he hesitates to take you around with him too much."

"Didn't he take Mrs. Matthews with him?"

"Who was she?"

"She was his secretary before I came. She'd been with him five years."

"What was she like?"

"Oh, nice. Middle-aged. White hair. Kindly. And I'm sure very efficient."

"No one his wife would worry about?"

"I'm sure not. She was older than they and married. Why? Do you think his wife would have been jealous of me?"

"No. Not jealous exactly. But I understand she was inclined to be possessive."

"That's strange. That's what Mrs. Matthews told me: that she was possessive. She also told me he was very much in love with her."

"Yes, I guess he was."

"Not that it's any of my business, but did you know them before you came to work for Mr. Randolph?"

"Yes and no."

"In other words, you'd rather not tell me."

"It wouldn't clarify matters any even if I did."

"Did you know Jason?"

The dance ended, and Doug came back to us. "It just dawned on me I haven't had any lunch," he said. "Mind if I join you?"

What could we say but, "Of course not," and make a place for him at our small table while he went to get his food?

While he was gone, Luke said, "Perhaps I'd better make my excuses and circulate."

"Not on my account." Then I smiled. "Unless you'd like to dance with Alicia."

He grinned. "She's a luscious armful, to say the least." He hurriedly finished his plate of food and stood up just as Doug returned, a well filled plate in one hand, a cup of coffee in the other. Luke whisked away his dishes. "Here, take my place. I think I'll make myself sociable for a while."

Doug didn't argue but sat down in Luke's place. Looking up at him, Doug said, "Be ready to go about five-thirty? Maybe we can drive Karen home."

Luke said, "I'll have the car at the front entrance at five-thirty," and sauntered away.

Doug began to eat as if he were starved. "About Christmas," he said: "if you'd rather not get mixed up with that, I'll understand."

"It isn't a case of getting mixed up with it, as you put it; it's just that I wonder if it's the right thing to do."

He took a sip of coffee. "If I knew for sure what had happened to her —" he said thoughtfully.

"I can imagine how you feel."

He put his cup down and stopped eating. Looking at me earnestly, he said, "You know, I've been wondering, do you think she could have left me deliberately?"

I stared at him for a moment, then said, "Oh no! Why would she do that? She loved you and you loved her, and you were so happy together."

He didn't answer immediately, and I asked, "Weren't you?"

"I thought we were. But I guess you can't ever be sure."

"Anyway, how could she disappear without leaving a trace, even if she wanted to?"

"I don't know. But people do disappear."

"Yes, so they say."

He sighed and began to eat. Then he said, "Well, there's no use getting you mixed up in it. I suppose I ought to take Vivienne out to dinner on Christmas. She always spent the day with us."

I didn't answer because, even though I

would have loved to spend Christmas with him, I didn't think I should. So that was that.

And it was just as well I didn't, because that was the day I received the telegram telling me my brother had been killed in action in Cambodia.

Christmas was on a Friday, so I called Doug at home the next day and told him, and he was very sympathetic. "I can't tell you how sorry I am. Of course you know if there's anything I can do to help, I will."

I said, "I know. And thank you." Then, just to be polite, I asked, "Did you have a nice Christmas?"

He didn't answer right away, then said, "Well, Vivienne insisted I have dinner with her in her apartment, and it was pleasant enough. She's a good cook, and she can be quite entertaining if she wants to."

I had no answer to that, so he added, "She gave me a plant she'd raised especially for me, a plant she said was good luck. It's a hyacinth."

I said, "Oh? Do you like hyacinths?"

He chuckled. "Never knew what one was before."

I said, "They smell nice, but they aren't my favorite flower."

"What is your favorite flower?"

"You probably won't believe this, but daisies are."

"Not roses or orchids or something like that?"

"No. Just plain field daisies. I love them."

"I'll have to get you some sometimes."

I laughed. "I used to go out in the fields and pick armfuls of them when we lived in Rye."

"You could probably do that on our island. I've never really noticed." Then he went on, "Well, again let me say how sorry I am about your brother, and let me know if there is anything I can do to help. And don't worry about coming into the office Monday. Don't come until you feel like it."

Suddenly I found myself crying, and in a shaky voice I said, "All right. And thank you." I hung up almost rudely before he could hear the sob in my voice.

Late that afternoon Luke came to the apartment with a large box of flowers. When I opened the box and saw they were daisies, tears came to my eyes. "Oh! How nice. But where could he get daisies in December."

Luke grinned. "You can get anything in this town if you know how and have the money." Then he said, "I'm very sorry about your brother. Is there anything I can do?"

I said, "Thank you; I don't believe there is

71

anything. It's just one of those things."
Then, remembering my manners, I said,
"Won't you sit down and have a cup of
coffee?"

He hesitated. "Thank you, but I have to
pick up the boss in half an hour. Some
couple has invited him to dinner."

Gradually Doug began to go out more.
Couples who had been friends of Ariadne's
and his invited him to dinner, and in turn he
entertained them. But as far as I knew, his
name was never linked with any other
woman.

He was friendly with me in the office, and
several times he and Luke drove me home
when it was storming, but our conversations
in the car were always impersonal. During
these trips Luke kept his place as the chauffeur, and although sometimes there was a
twinkle in his eyes as he touched the peak of
his cap and said, "Good evening, Miss
Foster," he never presumed again to display
the friendliness he had showed at the
Christmas party.

Vivienne kept away from the office, and if
I ever answered the phone when she called
Doug, she was polite but curt, all of which
suited me fine.

Doug never suggested taking me around

to the various factories with him, although he did say once, "I'll have to take you up to Hartford sometime. My father started that factory, and that is how I became interested in this business. When he died, he left me the business. And having majored in business management at Harvard and grown up in the midst of fabrics, you might say, I gradually formed what is now known as Amalgamated Fabrics, and they made me president."

And so the months slipped by. When the vacation list came around, Doug asked, "When do you want your vacation?"

I shrugged. "It doesn't really matter. I don't plan to do anything."

He shook his head. "You should," he said. "You should get away. You need a change."

I guess I sounded woebegone as I said, "Where would I go, all alone? My mother and I used to drive up to Cape Cod every summer, but I don't want to go there alone."

He gazed out of the window at the tall, many-windowed buildings in the distance. It was one of the rare smog-free days when they could be seen. "I know what you mean," he said. "I'll probably go up to the island for a few days from time to time, and then I have that trip to Europe to make in August for the World Trade Association. They want me to attend several meetings concerning fabrics."

I said, "Yes. That will be nice for you."

He sat thinking for a few minutes; then he gave me a sudden look. "How would you like to go up to Sanctuary for the two weeks I'm abroad? There won't be anybody there except the servants, and you can just relax and swim and boat and skin dive, if that interests you. There's all the equipment in the boathouse."

"Oh, I couldn't do that!" I cried.

"Why not?"

"I'd feel funny. And people would think it was —"

"Oh, *people!*" he exploded. "Who's going to know? I won't be there."

"Just the same —"

He sighed and shrugged. "Well, it was just an idea. Think it over. If you change your mind, let me know."

I said, "Thank you," and hurried to my office. It was silly of me to feel embarrassed, but those darned bells were beginning to ring again.

Well, to make a long story short, in the end that was what I did with my vacation in August. Doug flew to Europe for his business meetings several days before I left for the island of Sanctuary in Lake Tranquil.

If I had known Vivienne was going to be there, I most certainly would not have gone.

Chapter Four

But to get back to the present, here I was on the island of Sanctuary, and it was too late to change my mind. As I stood watching Luke fastening the boat to the pier, I realized he hadn't noticed my reaction to the news that Vivienne was there. And to be realistic about it, why should he care, one way or another? He finished securing the boat, then led me through the boathouse, which looked more like a mystic sitting room, evidently for the users of the boats. From an open door I could see a house that looked like a large studio. Luke said, "That's the living room. You'll find Vivienne there waiting for you. I'll take your bags to your bedroom. You can go there later."

I said, "Thank you," and left him, going over to the building he had told me was the living room of this strange complex. The door was open, but a screen door was closed and hooked. Inside the room, I could see Vivienne. She was watering something in a flowerpot over by a window, but whatever it was, it hadn't grown above the soil yet. I decided it must be a bulb of some sort. She had her back to the door and seemed to be talking to the flowerpot. Listening, I heard her say:

"As the root grows
"And this blossom blows,
"May his heart be turned to me.
"As my will, so mote it be!"

I thought, "What a strange thing to be saying to a flowerpot." I wondered if I should knock to let her know I was there. But before I had decided what to do, she turned and saw me. "Oh, Karen," she said. "I didn't expect you quite yet."

I said, "I guess the bus made good time. May I come in?"

"Of course." She put the watering can to one side and came over to unhook the screen door.

As I entered the room, and merely for the sake of making conversation, I said, "What are you growing?"

She smiled, and her face lit up. "Hyacinths," she said.

I thought, "One of those again." A hyacinth for Doug for Christmas, and now another one. Was it Doug she was casting the spell on? I had to say something, so I said. "Oh, really? I like hyacinths."

"They are a flower of love," she told me. "Maybe some day I'll teach you how to cast a hyacinth spell."

I laughed. "Would it get me anything?" I asked facetiously.

She shrugged. "Maybe the man you love."

This surprised me, because I had never thought of Vivienne in connection with love. Yet she was certainly young enough for it, only twenty-seven, the same age as her twin sister would be if she was still alive.

"But enough of that," Vivienne said. "I'm forgetting my duties as hostess. Welcome to Sanctuary." But there was no welcome in her eyes. Now the smile was gone, and there was just a blankness that made me feel cold, even though the afternoon was warm.

She was wearing a gray dress of a thin, floating material, with a high neck and long sleeves and a long full skirt. Around her neck was a heavy silver chain with a pendant of a peculiar stone outlined in silver. I think it was a moonstone, and the shape of it was quite unusual. On her left wrist was a wide silver bracelet which had a matching stone set in it.

She motioned me to a grouping of furniture. "But sit down. You must be tired. It's a long trip up here."

I said, "Oh, it's not so bad," and glanced around the most beautiful room I had ever seen. I'd noticed from the outside that it was a two-story room with enormous windows at each end. The glass panes were left uncovered, but there were white drapes at each side, framing the windows without obstructing the light or the view. The building was turned and the shoreline curved so that the view from all the windows was of the lake. Modernistic furniture was arranged in conversation groups in various parts of the enormous, Gothic-domed room. The color scheme was oyster white with touches of black and an occasional pillow of flame orange. There was white wall-to-wall carpeting, as soft as down to step on, and spotlessly clean. By one of the end windows was a white concert grand piano, and in the middle of each side wall was a large white marble fireplace with teakwood carvings and black candles on the mantels.

Vivienne asked, "Like it?"

"It's beautiful! breathtaking!"

Vivienne smiled, rather smugly, I thought. "Ariadne and I designed it and selected the furniture. We planned the entire place, for that matter."

I made the mistake of asking, "Didn't Mr. Randolph have any hand in it?" Even as I asked, I knew he couldn't have. It didn't look like him. But then, neither did the house in the city.

At my question, Vivienne's eyes seemed to glaze over and become more expressionless than usual. She said, "Douglas is only interested in his work." She always called him Douglas, never Doug the way everyone else did. She walked, or to be more exact, floated across the room to a grouping of chairs, a sofa and a low round glass table. "But come and sit down. Tea will be along in a few minutes." She sat down on the white velvet sofa, and I followed and chose a tufted black satin scoop chair near her, with the glass table between us. I had the feeling that I would always want to have something between Vivienne and myself.

After we were settled in our seats, I didn't know what to say. Having Vivienne acting as hostess made me uncomfortable and embarrassed. When Doug had suggested I come up there, it had been because, as I understood it, the place was going to be empty, with the exception of the servants, for the two weeks he would be in Europe as a good will ambassador of the World Trade Association; and, according to him, he would rather have someone there than have the place untenanted.

Sitting facing Vivienne now across the glass table, I scrutinized her face. I'd never taken a really good look at her before. Now I tried to find a resemblance to her sister in her face. It was there, but very remotely. Her nose was broader than Ariadne's had been and her lips thicker. Her eyes were not the vivid blue of Ariadne's, but paler and smaller. Ariadne's skin had had a glow to it, fair though it was, perhaps because although she had spent many hours at the piano, she had also spent a great deal of time outdoors. She used to play golf, ride horseback in Central Park every morning when the weather was good and they were in the city, swum, sailed and done a lot of walking. Vivienne, on the other hand, spent most of her time indoors. She read a great deal and belonged to various clubs and societies that kept her indoors going to meetings and lectures. Mrs. Matthews had told me that.

There was a knock on the side of the screen door, and a middle-aged woman came in. She had a swarthy complexion and graying black hair bobbed and hanging around her rather flabby face. Her eyes were black and darted from Vivienne to me in a questioning way. She had on a pants suit of dark green which seemed to be too big for her and a large silver and turquoise medallion hanging around her neck. She smiled and disclosed yellowed, uneven teeth. "May I join you?" she asked.

Vivienne looked annoyed but said, "Of course." Then she introduced us. "Mrs. Davis, this is Miss Foster, Douglas' secretary."

The woman looked me over carefully as she said, "How do you do?" She came and sat down beside Vivienne.

I said, "How do you do, Mrs. Davis." I noticed her hands, though fattish, had a look of strength to them, and the nails were painted a vivid red, with the enamel chipped off in places.

Just then a maid came in, rolling a double-decked tray such as they use in hotels for room service. Vivienne said, "Thank you, Lisbeth."

The maid began arranging a silver tea service and plates of tiny sandwiches and cakes on the glass table. While she was doing that, Vivienne, Mrs. Davis and I sat silently watching her. When everything was in place and the maid had left, taking the now empty rolling tray with her, Vivienne began to pour the tea, saying, "Each of these buildings is without steps, as you will notice. That is so food can be brought from the kitchen to any of the buildings if anyone doesn't feel like going to the dining room."

I took the cup of tea she leaned across the table to give me, saying, "Whose idea was it to have each room in a separate building?"

"Ariadne's, really, although I helped her with the place. You see, when we lived together in the city, before Ariadne married, we used to say that people shouldn't have to live so close together, as they do in an apartment or even a house. And one day Ariadne said, 'If I had my way, I'd build a house with separate rooms — really separate — each in a different building.' We laughed about it at the time, but the seed of the idea had been planted, and when Douglas bought the land up here on this island, intending to build a summer place, Ariadne remembered her idea about a house with each room in a separate building. When she told Douglas about it, he laughed, thought about it, then said, 'You know, that might be a good idea. Go ahead and try it if you want to.' " She passed me a plate of sandwiches, which turned out to be cucumber and watercress. I took one and watched her take one. I noticed that her hands, though well cared for, reminded me of talons. They were not graceful and feminine the way Ariadne's had been. I asked, "Do you play the piano?"

She said, "No. I used to sing a little, but I

don't any more." Then she looked me directly in the eyes for a moment, and I saw sparks in them as I had that day in the office. "Why did you come up here?" she asked.

Taken by surprise, I almost dropped my cup of tea. "Why, because, that is, Doug invited me and —"

"Since when have you and my brother-in-law become such good friends?"

I hesitated. "Well, after all, I *am* his private secretary."

"That doesn't give you the right to impose on his good nature and privacy."

"Privacy? In what way am I imposing on his privacy by accepting his invitation to spend my vacation here, when he isn't even going to be here?"

Her sparkling eyes challenged me. "Well, I'm just warning you, don't start snooping around."

While we were talking, Mrs. Davis was eating and drinking her tea, seemingly not paying any attention to us. Now she said, "Come now, Viv. I'm sure Miss Foster has no intention of snooping."

I gave myself a little shake to break the spell Vivienne's eyes were beginning to cast over me. "I have no intention of snooping," I said. "All I want to do is relax: swim, sit out in the sun, walk in the fresh air and maybe spend some time on the lake. Luke said he would show me how to run the launch."

"Luke takes too much on himself. At least Jason minded his own business and kept his place. Poor man. Douglas should never have let him go."

Mrs. Davis made a clicking sound with her tongue.

I nibbled at a sandwich for a moment, although I'd suddenly lost my appetite. Then I said, "If I had known you were going to be here, I would not have come."

"What do you mean by that?"

I met her eyes and saw the sparks were disappearing, and I was reminded again of spent skyrockets. I said, "When Doug invited me to come up here, he made me to understand the place would be untenanted except for the servants. If he had expected you to be here, I think he would have mentioned it."

She looked down into her teacup. "Are you implying that I have no right to be here?"

"Not at all. I am sure you are always welcome in any home of Doug's."

"Yes," she said, and kept looking down into her teacup. Then she said, "However, there is no need for him ever to know I was here at this time."

"Then he doesn't know you are here?" It was none of my business, of course, but something made me want to ferret out her exact meaning.

Her lips tightened. She glanced over at the white piano silhouetted against the large window at the end of the room, and I tried to visualize Ariadne sitting there, playing. "I do not feel I have to account to him for every move I make!" she said almost viciously.

"Even when you are staying in his house?" I hated myself for bugging her, but something seemed to drive me on.

She said, "I shall only be here until tomorrow; then you can have the whole place to yourself."

"I don't want the whole place to myself," I told her. "There certainly seems to be enough territory for two people to be here at the same time without getting in each other's way. But spending my vacation in the vicinity of someone who is as plainly antagonistic toward me as you are isn't exactly my idea of a vacation."

She seemed to become less tense then than she had been. She leaned back and sipped her tea. "I am not antagonistic toward you. As a matter of fact, I have no feeling toward you one way or the other. But I am warning you — mind your own business. I expect to have some friends here this evening, but there will be no reason for you to fraternize with them. You go your way, and we will go ours."

"That will suit me fine," I told her.

Mrs. Davis suddenly stopped eating. "You know, Viv," she said, "Miss Foster might like to meet some of our friends."

"Oh, don't be ridiculous!" Vivienne said crossly.

Mrs. Davis sucked her teeth noisily. "We could use some youth in our group," she said.

"Shut up, will you, Carry?" Vivienne snapped at her.

I put down my cup and saucer on the glass table, finished the dainty sandwich which I no longer wanted, and stood up. "And now, if I may, I would like to go to my room, wherever it is," I told Vivienne.

She got up and touched a bell at the side of one of the fireplaces. "Just wait outside," she told me tonelessly, "and Lisbeth will come and take you to your room." She went over to the entrance and held open the screen door until I walked over and went out. Then she hooked it. Mrs. Davis stayed on the sofa. The last I saw of her, she was scratching her head. Then Vivienne closed the door with a finality that sent a chill up my back.

I was glad to see Lisbeth hurrying along one of the flower-bordered paths as she came from one of the back buildings, presumably the kitchen.

Chapter Five

The room Lisbeth led me to was like a picture in *House Beautiful*. It, like the living room, was two stories high, with a Gothic ceiling and large arched windows. The king-size bed was on a platform, like a throne, and it had a draped canopy of white silk and a white silk spread embroidered in gold with a pattern of the signs of the zodiac. The color scheme of the room was apple green and jonquil yellow. The wall-to-wall carpet was a pale green, and when you walked on it you felt as if you were walking on moss. The drapes were yellow, the furniture an oyster white, with chair cushions in either green or yellow.

Lisbeth began going around the room. She rolled back a pair of mirrored doors onto a closet where I saw my clothes were hanging. "I took the liberty of unpacking for you," she said.

I said, "Thank you."

She went to another mirrored door in the corner of the room, opened it and showed me a lavatory with a hand basin, a john and a glassed-in shower. The color scheme reflected that of the bedroom: apple green and jonquil yellow with towels in each color. She said, "Each bedroom has its own lavatory, but there is a large bathroom in building ten. That is back toward the woods."

I gave a sigh of relief, because I wouldn't have liked the idea of having to go to another building for a bath or other necessities that might occur in the night.

There was a portable TV on a rolling stand at one side of the bedroom. She said, "This works this way," and began snapping buttons and turning dials. I watched her, said, "I see," and she went to a large white bureau which had tracings of the signs of the zodiac in gold on the front of the drawers. Opening the top drawer, she said, "I put your underwear, scarves and things like that in these drawers."

There was a white clock radio on a white bedside table together with a reading lamp. Going to a piece of furniture that looked like a chest of drawers, Lisbeth opened up doors, disclosing a completely equipped liquor cabinet. "Just in case you want to fix yourself a drink," she explained. "The ice cubes are here." And she showed me a small refrigerator built into the side of the cabinet.

I couldn't help smiling. "All the comforts of home," I said.

She smiled. She was a pretty girl, about twenty. She had soft brown curly hair, cut in a close cap style that framed her high cheek-boned face. Her eyes were a sherry brown and sparkled when she smiled, and she had very pretty, even white teeth. "If there's anything you want and don't have here in the room, all you have to do is phone the kitchen." She went over to a white flat-topped desk at the side of the room where there were two princess phones: one apple green, the other yellow. "The green one is for outside calls," she explained; "the yellow is a house phone." Taking a small white-covered book from a drawer of the desk, she explained, "In this you will find a listing and a chart of the different rooms."

She smiled at me pityingly, I thought, and said, "I guess that's all. Dinner will be served in the dining room — that's building six — at seven o'clock. Or if you prefer, I can have a tray brought here for you."

I said, "I think tonight I'd like that."

She smiled brightly. "Okay. Bye now." She went out.

I glanced at my wrist watch. It was nearly five o'clock, and suddenly I discovered I was very tired. The trip up from the city had been interesting but tiring, and the tea with Vivienne hadn't helped any. I decided to undress, take a shower and put on fresh clothes for dinner, even though I would be dining alone in my room.

As I began taking off my clothes, I wandered around the room and looked out of the windows. There weren't as many windows in this room as there were in the living room; two at one end and one on each side. The ones at the end looked out on the lake; the side windows faced other buildings. But there was ample space between each building so there was no feeling of being shut in, and the flowers that bordered the paths were beautiful. Colors ran rampant through them, and every flower I had ever heard of was represented.

The room was comfortably cool in spite of the heat outside, as the living room had been, and I decided the buildings must be air-conditioned, although there was no sight or sound to indicate it.

I didn't know how I should dress for my solitary dinner, so I finally chose a pale pink pants suit with a tunic that zipped up the front to a mandarin collar. It was a little dressy, but I might as well pretend I was having a gala evening even though I wasn't. The thought flashed through my mind that it would be nice if Doug were there. But I immediately squashed that. Thoughts like that were dangerous to my peace of mind.

My hair is black, quite thick, with a natural wave, and I brushed the front of it back from my face and the rest of it out to its full shoulder length. Then I took the sides, drew them to the top of my head and stuck combs in to hold the waves in place. The rest of it hung freely down my back. I loosened a strand on each side of my face so it would come down in front of each ear. I put on blue eye shadow and darkened my lashes to deepen the gray blue of my eyes. Pink strap sandals over the sheerest of stockings completed my outfit. You'd have thought I was going to some swank night club.

By the time I was finished, it was a quarter to six. I decided I'd have a couple of cocktails and mixed some martinis; then I turned on the TV and relaxed in a comfortable chair to enjoy my cocktails and watch the six o'clock news.

The news had progressed through Vietnam, strikes, political squabbles in Washington and disagreements at the U.N., when suddenly a large plane was shown landing at an airfield in Brussels. And the first person out of it, appearing at the door and coming down the steps to the field where a semicircle of reporters were waiting, was my boss, Douglas Randolph. I almost choked on my cocktail, sat up straight on my chair and leaned forward. Doug waved his right arm and seemed to be looking directly at me, and I had to hold in the "Hi" I was on the verge of saying. Then he greeted the reporters with a smile, and a half-dozen mikes were thrust in his face. "Mr. Randolph," one of the reporters called, "why have you come to Brussels at this time?"

Into the microphone he said, "For several business meetings for the World Trade Association."

"You haven't come on your honeymoon?" another reporter asked.

Doug smiled and pretended to look around him. "Do you see anybody with me?" he asked.

The man said, "No. But the lady may still be in the plane."

Doug frowned. "That's nonsense!" he said.

"Has it ever been established what happened to your first wife?" another man asked.

"No! And what do you mean, my *first* wife? I have had only one wife, and as far as I know I am still married to her!"

"Then you don't believe she's dead?" the man asked.

Doug's lips tightened, and the cleft in his

chin deepened. "I do not want to believe that!" he said grimly.

"If you were sure she was dead, would you marry again?" The question came from a woman reporter.

Doug said, "I do not know. And now, if you will excuse me, I would like to get to my hotel." He pushed his way through the crowd, his face grim, his shoulders squared. The woman reporter called after him, "Is it true you are in love with your secretary?"

I gasped, then held my breath. But if Doug heard the question, he chose to ignore it. He strode across the field to a long black car that had evidently been sent to meet him, got in and was whisked away; and the TV switched to a ball game already in progress.

I turned off the TV, got up and began pacing back and forth the length of the room, sipping my cocktail as I went. When I'd drained the glass, I stopped at the liquor cabinet and poured myself another.

I wondered if Vivienne had been watching the TV news. If she had, the woman reporter's last question was not going to make my life on the island of Sanctuary any easier.

I also wondered if the servants in the kitchen had heard the question. Had Luke?

Desperately I wished I knew how to run the launch. If I had, I'd have gotten into it and gone to the farthest end of the lake. Or I'd have stayed out on it all night. Or perhaps I'd have gone to the inn for the night and taken the bus back to the city in the morning.

Whatever had prompted that woman reporter to ask such a question? How did she know anything about me? I was sure I had kept my feelings well hidden in the office. And surely, even if Doug was the least bit interested in me personally, which he wasn't, *he* had kept it well hidden, too. So who had talked? And how had the idea spread way across the ocean and part of a continent to Brussels?

I stopped my pacing and stood gazing out of the window overlooking the lake. It was beginning to get dark, even though it was only a little after six. It must be because of the mountain over on the mainland in the near distance. The sun had gradually slid behind it, and instantly the shadows on the lake had deepened.

Then, as I watched, I saw a boat slide alongside the pier beside the boathouse, and two men and a woman stepped out onto the pier. One of the men was leading a large dog by a rope. Dog? No, that wasn't a dog. It looked more like a goat. But why a goat? And were the people some of Vivienne's expected guests?

Perhaps I could see better when they came closer. But they weren't coming any closer. They were going around the boat-house and back by the woods, so instead of seeing them better I lost sight of them entirely. Their boat left as soon as they disappeared.

I finished the rest of my drink and sat down to wait for my dinner. The vacation I had looked forward to was beginning to take on the overtones of an unpleasant experience.

Whether or not Doug had realized his arrival at the Brussels airport would be televised back to the states I did not know. But one way or another, I was going to feel very embarrassed when I had to meet him face to face again. Also, I would be embarrassed when my vacation was over and I had to return to the office.

When the door chime sounded, I jumped up to open the door, thinking it was one of the servants with my dinner. So I was surprised to see Luke standing there. He asked, "Busy?"

"No." I glanced around the room, wondering if it would be all right to invite him

97

in. After all, it was a bedroom.

Sensing my thought, he smiled. "I was just wondering," he said. "I understand Vivienne is having guests this evening. That will leave you all alone, and I thought perhaps you'd like to go over to the movie house. Believe it or not, they are showing *Gone With the Wind.*"

"Really?"

I couldn't help smiling. "And now I'll tell *you* something. Believe it or not, I've never seen *Gone With the Wind.*"

He threw back his head and laughed. "Then that settles it," he said. "No girl's education is complete until she's seen *Gone With the Wind.*"

"Okay. When do we start?"

"Have you eaten yet?"

"No. Lisbeth said somebody would bring my dinner here at seven."

He surveyed me thoughtfully for a moment. Then he said, "You're looking too pretty to sit here and eat all alone. What say we hop in one of the boats and go over to the mainland for a bite? The Inn has very good food."

"Can I go like this?"

"Why not?"

"Oh — well, I don't know how they dress up here."

"Just like they do down in the city."

For the first time I noticed that he had changed his clothes from the dungarees and sweater he'd worn when he had met me in the afternoon to gray slacks, a white shirt open at the neck, with a gay scarf around his strong browned throat, and a light blue blazer with brass buttons. As I stood there in the doorway, I could feel that with the disappearance of the sun behind the mountain, the crystal-clear air had turned cooler.

"Hadn't I better tell the kitchen I'm eating out?" I asked him.

"I suppose so. Just phone over. Dial 12 on the house phone."

I went over to the desk and, using the yellow phone, pushed the button marked 12. In a moment a woman answered, "Kitchen."

I said, "This is Miss Foster. I just wanted to tell you not to bother with dinner for me tonight. I'm dining out."

The woman said, "Very well, Miss Foster," and hung up.

While I was at the phone, Luke had been looking around the room. When I turned away from the phone, he said, "I've never seen the inside of this room before. It's really something, isn't it?"

I said, "Yes, it is."

He said, "You know this was Mrs. Randolph's room, don't you?"

I couldn't answer right away, because the information had given me a jolt. To cover my embarrassment, I went over to the bureau, found my white summer purse and began putting into it makeup, money, credit cards, etc. When I'd finished I said, "No, I didn't. I wonder if I should be in here?"

"Why not?"

"Well, I wonder if Doug would want anyone to use it?"

"I don't think he'd want just *anyone* in it. But you're not just anyone."

I whirled around, taken by surprise. "Just what do you mean by that?" I demanded.

He smiled. "Oh, come now. As if you didn't know."

I walked over to him and looked him right in the eyes. "No, I don't know," I told him. I was trembling with sudden anger. Or was it fright? I felt as if things were closing in on me — unseen, intangible things; things with which I couldn't cope. But before I could say any more, Luke advised, "You'd better bring a coat or a sweater. It will get cooler when the sun goes down."

I went to the closet, rolled back one of the mirrored doors and took out a short white wool coat.

Luke asked, "Are those her clothes?"

I closed the door too quickly. It slammed, and for a moment I held my breath, fearing the mirror would crack. But it didn't. Over my shoulder I said, "No! They are mine. There are no personal possessions belonging to anyone else anywhere in the room."

Luke raised his eyebrows but made no comment. Suddenly I didn't want to go out with him. But neither did I want to stay alone in the room, particularly now I knew it had been Ariadne's room. Why had I been assigned to it? I wondered. Was it one of Vivienne's ideas, or had Doug given orders that I was to be put in it?

Luke asked, "All set?" and I had no choice but to say, "Yes, I guess so."

We left the room, and as I was closing the door I asked, "I wonder if I should lock the door?"

"I don't think anyone else does."

So I just closed it and followed Luke along the flower-bordered path. It was only a short walk to the boathouse, and when we reached there I saw it was brightly lighted inside. Luke helped me onto the same boat in which he'd brought me from the mainland in the afternoon, untied it and jumped aboard himself. Working at the dial board in the bow, he said, "Now watch how I start it."

It seemed a simple operation, comparable to starting a car. When he had the boat backed out, turned around and headed out into the lake, he said, "Why did you come up here?"

Taken by surprise, I didn't know how to answer him. So he went on, "Don't you know what this place is?"

"Why — er — it's a summer place," I stammered.

The boat was gliding over the calm waters of the lake at a comfortable speed, and I looked around me. The island we were leaving and the shores of the mainland were now darkening masses where lights were beginning to appear, like stars coming into an early evening sky.

"Mind if I give you a little fatherly advice?" Luke asked.

"That depends," I countered.

Without looking at me, he said, "Go home. Go back to the city on the bus in the morning. I'd say go back tonight, but there is only one bus a day, unless I drive you down tonight. The cadillac is parked in the garage back of the inn."

I felt a cold chill sliding over me, as if something evil were creeping nearer. But it was probably just because a cool breeze was starting up. I pulled my coat closer around me as I said, "I don't understand. I just got here. Why should I go right home?"

Luke steered the boat out to the center of the lake, then turned it so that I could see the lights of the inn down at the end of the lake. He said, "Because you're not safe here."

"Why not?"

He didn't speak for a long time, and I began to think he wasn't going to. Suddenly he asked, "Know anything about witches?"

I laughed. "Witches? Heavens, no!"

"Then get away from here, and get away quickly before you find out."

"What on earth are you talking about?" I asked, noticing how broad his shoulders were as he stood there at the helm of the boat with his back to me.

Suddenly he asked, "How long have you worked for Douglas Randolph?"

"A little over a year."

"And you never knew his wife and her sister were witches?"

"Are you crazy, or are you just putting me on?"

"Neither. I'm telling you. Sanctuary is a witches' haven. The whole place is laid out according to their beliefs. They hold covens at the full of the moon, back in the woods. What do you think Vivienne is doing tonight — she and her so-called friends?"

"How should I know what she's doing? Having a dinner party, I presume. So what?"

"So after dinner, they'll go back into the woods, take off their clothes and hold a coven. Today is August 1st. They call it Lamas Day, and they perform a weird ceremony and make sacrifices."

I jumped to my feet and grabbed Luke's arm. "The goat!" I cried.

He turned his head and looked at me. "Goat?" he repeated.

I said, "Yes. Goat! I saw two men and a woman arrive, and one of the men had an animal on a rope. At first I thought it was a big dog; then I realized it was a goat."

"Probably slit its throat."

I gasped. "Oh, no!"

"That's part of the ritual."

"Can't we stop them?"

"Not without letting them know we're on to them and maybe getting our own throats slit."

"Oh, but they wouldn't dare do that!"

"Wouldn't they? What do you think happened to Ariadne?"

I was beginning to shiver. "Oh, no! But

she was Vivienne's sister! She wouldn't kill her own sister!"

"Maybe *she* wouldn't, but there are others who might."

"I can't believe it."

"Haven't you heard of Satanism?"

"Only in books like *Rosemary's Baby*. And certainly I don't believe it exists."

"Well, you'd better start believing it."

"Does Doug know about this place and what goes on here?"

"No, I'm sure he doesn't."

"Did he know Ariadne was a witch?"

"Of course not. They keep it all very quiet."

"What about the signs of the zodiac in her room?"

"That could pass for an interest in astrology. That's harmless enough."

"And the signs are decorative."

"That too."

"How come you know so much about all of this? You've worked for Doug for less than a year, and I've been with him longer than that."

He didn't answer me for a long moment; then he said, "Well, maybe I'll tell you — but not yet."

For the rest of the trip over to the mainland, we didn't talk. I wondered if he had heard the six o'clock news but hesitated to ask. Should I take his advice and go home tonight or the first thing in the morning? My common sense told me to go, but my curiosity was prompting me to stay. If I could see what went on at that coven tonight, I could warn Doug, and he would do something about it. Also, if he knew what was going on, it might give him a lead in discovering what had happened to Ariadne. Not that I wanted him to discover that his wife had been killed by her sister or her sister's friends. But if he actually knew she was dead, he wouldn't keep on hoping that some day she would come back.

Then, after thinking that over for a few moments, I realized that since that woman reporter's question on the newscast, I couldn't be the one to discover the truth about Ariadne. Perhaps she was alive and in hiding somewhere. Or perhaps she was being held a prisoner. Was Vivienne evil enough to have her sister abducted so she could have her husband? But she would never get Doug under any circumstances, no matter how many hyacinth spells she cast. Of that I was sure. But maybe having him all to herself the way she had this past year was enough for her. After all, she'd lived in the city house with him for several

106

months after Ariadne had disappeared. And now here she was ensconced on Sanctuary as if she owned the place. And in a couple of weeks Doug would be back from Europe and come up here.

Breaking into my confused thoughts, Luke said, "Well, here we are." He brought the boat smoothly beside the pier, throttled the motor, threw a line over a post on the pier, tied it, then turned to me. "Come on. I'm starved, and I can smell that good food over at the inn."

I took the hand he held out to me, and together we stepped up onto the pier. I asked, "Is this the only place to dock on the mainland?"

"Oh no. There are places on the opposite side of the lake and down at the other end, but we never use them."

"But Vivienne's friends could use them so people around here wouldn't see them?"

He shrugged. "I suppose so."

When we went into the inn dining room, I discovered Luke had phoned ahead for a reservation. To the head waiter who met us at the door, he said, "A reservation for two for Mr. Mansfield." It was the first time I had heard his last name, and it came as a surprise. As a matter of fact, I'd never thought of him as having a last name. I used to make out Jason's salary check, but Doug had been taking care of paying Luke himself.

We were ushered to a table for two by a window that overlooked the lake, and when we were seated Luke asked, "What would you like to drink?"

I hesitated. I wasn't much of a drinker, and I'd already had two martinis. When I said, "Could I just have tomato juice? I had a couple of martinis while I was watching the news," he gave me a quick look. Then he said to the waiter, "One tomato juice and one Scotch on the rocks." As soon as the waiter left us, he asked, "So you heard?"

I felt my face getting warm, and quick tears came to my eyes. All I could do was nod my head. There was a goblet of ice water at my place, and I reached for it, took a sip and put it down, but not before my shaking hand had spilled some of the water.

Luke gazed out of the window so he wouldn't have to look at me. "I was hoping you wouldn't," he said.

After a moment, when I could trust my voice, I asked, "What am I going to do? It's so embarrassing."

He turned his head and looked at me, and his eyes were kindly. "It's none of my business, I know, but is there any truth to it?"

Gritting my teeth, which I suddenly discovered were chattering, I said, "None whatever!"

The waiter brought our drinks and placed them before us. Luke picked up his and, moving aside my tomato juice, put the Scotch on the rocks in front of me. To the waiter he said, "Bring another of these."

The waiter said, "Yes, sir," and hurried away, and Luke ordered me, "Drink that. You need it."

Docilely I obeyed him and was grateful. The warmth of the amber liquid stopped the chattering of my teeth, and I was able to relax a little.

Luke said, "Don't let it throw you. I don't think he even heard that fool woman's last question."

"But everybody watching the news broadcast did, and that includes probably everybody who works for Amalgamated Fabrics, Inc."

He smiled slightly and shook his head. "Probably not. They would be on their way home at that time; not watching television."

"All I need is for just one person in the firm to have seen and heard it, and it will be all over the company, including the general offices and all of the outlying factories."

The waiter brought his drink, and he took

a sip of it. "There would be one way to scotch the idea." He held up his drink and smiled. "If you'll pardon the pun."

I asked, "What?"

"Get married to somebody else."

"But I don't know anybody else. That is, I'm not going out with anyone in particular." I was so taken by surprise I answered him honestly without thinking.

"How about me?"

I gasped and stared at him. I thought he was joking, but he wasn't. His face was serious, and for the first time I realized he was handsome, not just another man, as I'd always thought him. *"You?"* I cried, louder than I'd meant to.

He looked down at his drink. "Oh, I know I'm only the chauffeur, and if you have your eyes on the boss I'm not much of a substitute, but —" He gulped down his drink all at once and motioned to a waiter to bring him another. Then he looked at me and forced me to meet his eyes. "I've always admired you," he said. "And I don't always have to be a chauffeur. As a matter of fact, I never was before, and I have a law degree, if I want to use it again."

I stared at him. "Law degree?" I asked. "Then why on earth are you acting as a chauffeur?"

He smiled ruefully. "Shall we say — force of circumstances?"

I sipped my drink and looked out of the window. How could I answer him? He was offering me refuge from a very embarrassing situation. But a marriage had to be based on more than a transitory arrangement of convenience. I didn't even know him, or he me.

Seeing my dilemma, he said, "Never mind. Forget it. I guess I spoke out of turn. But just remember this: if there is ever anything I can do to help or make things easier for you, just let me know."

I turned my head and looked at him then. "I don't know what to say. You are very kind, but — well, we scarcely know each other."

The waiter came and asked if we'd like to order our dinner, and Luke said, "Yes, I guess we'd better," and took the large menu card the waiter handed him. Making our selections helped bridge the awkwardness of the moment, and we both took longer than was necessary. But the waiter was pleasant about it, and when we'd finished he suggested a New York State champagne for which the locality was noted.

When he left us I said, "I want to see that coven tonight."

Luke shook his head, and his brow

furrowed. "That wouldn't be wise," he told me.

"But if it's held back in the woods, couldn't I hide somewhere? They wouldn't even know I was there."

He kept shaking his head. "If you were discovered, your life wouldn't be worth a plugged nickel."

"I won't be discovered. It will be dark, except for the moon, and I will keep in the shadows."

"You won't like what you see."

"Maybe I'll learn something."

"You're better off not knowing."

"Please, Luke, I *have* to. Can't you understand? Maybe I'll learn something that will help Doug."

He looked at me sternly, and there was anger in his eyes. "You like him so much?" he asked with tight lips. "Enough to endanger your life?"

I finished my drink. I needed its warmth again. "Aren't you exaggerating?" I asked impatiently. "This is the United States, and this is the year 1971. We don't burn witches any more."

"That's right. But they have become a strong force these last few years. To some people who hold covens and sabbats in the living rooms of their expensive suburban houses, it may be just a fad. To others, such as these people, it is a religion." Then he added, "A backward religion, if you like. That's the way they say the Lord's Prayer — backward."

"How come you know so much about it?" I asked.

He shrugged. "I read. There are lots of books on the subject."

"If you know so much about them, what does coven mean?"

"Well, coven is derived from the Latin noun *conventus*. It is the same root from which we get our words covenant, convention, convent and convene."

I watched him as he talked. He was very serious. He went on, "As I understand it, there may be as many as three leaders in a coven: one god, one goddess and an initiator. The male leader represents the masculine power and generally takes first place; the female, the feminine, second; and the second male executor, or officer, third. Different covens have different titles for their leaders. In a coven that stresses love and fertility, they perform their rituals naked.

"The high priest may wear upon his head a shamanic horned helmet, or a mask covering his whole head and representing one of the coven's totem animals; a goat, ram, horse or whatever. The robes can vary in color, but black is preferred."

"I still can't understand why you are so interested in it."

He didn't answer me for a long moment; then he said, "Because I was once in love with Ariadne. Only her name was Helen then. She took the name of Ariadne when she became a witch."

"Did she become a witch before or after she married Doug?"

"Before. He doesn't even know her name was originally Helen."

"What made her choose the name of Ariadne?"

"Well, as I understand it, they are led by their astrological birth signs and planets. So I looked up the legends surrounding them and found that a female witch, born under Taurus as she was, her birthday being April 23rd, was ruled by Venus. That was evidently why she took the name Ariadne, who was the daughter of King Minos and Theseus' bride. The name Ariadne is a form of Aradia, who was one of the chief spirit powers of the witch world."

I said, "Very interesting. Then you knew Vivienne, too, before Ariadne married Doug?"

"No. My friendship with Helen was something Vivienne — her name was Anna then — didn't know anything about."

"But how could that be?"

"Well, at one time I had aspirations to become a violinist. We met at Juilliard."

"A violinist!" I exclaimed. "One minute you're a lawyer, the next a violinist. And now you're a chauffeur."

He began to smile. "I don't wonder you're confused," he said. "But here's our dinner. I'll straighten you out later."

"Just one more thing. How did Anna get the name Vivienne?"

"Well, many of them choose names of the legendary practitioners of the black arts. In the female list are Morgana, Armida, Vivienne, Melusina and many others. I don't know where Vivienne fits in, but she was one of them."

I said, "I see," but I didn't see at all. Anyway, we stopped talking while the waiter served us, and when he left we ate, mostly in silence. I guess the meal was delicious, but I didn't remember a thing about it. I ate it without tasting it. And I drank the champagne, which, on top of the martinis and the Scotch on the rocks, didn't help to clarify my mind.

After dinner, Luke insisted we go to the movie, promising that it would be out early enough for us to make it back to Sanctuary in time for me to see the coven, if that was what I wanted to do.

Like the dinner, I guess the movie was all right, but I don't remember much about it. Part of the time Luke held my hand, but I was scarcely aware of it. You've heard of people having a one-track mind. Well, that was the condition of my mind that evening. All I was interested in was seeing that coven, seeing what went on there and who the people were who took part.

Chapter Six

On the way back to Sanctuary after the movie, Luke said, "You'd better put on something dark before you go prowling around in the woods."

I agreed. "Yes, I guess so." Then I asked, "Will you come with me?"

"No!" The answer was sharp and firm.

"Will you tell me how to get to the right place?"

"Yes, I'll do that. I'll show you a round-about way. Otherwise you're apt to run into some of the participants, and then you'd never get there."

"You make them sound like Mafia murderers."

"No, they're not that bad. But they don't like to be found out. A pledge to keep their secret is one of their initiation oaths."

When the boat slid up beside the pier on Sanctuary, the lights in the boathouse were out, and the building was pitch dark. But Luke had a flashlight which he used so we could see to step out onto the pier. Then he said to me, "Stand still, and I'll put on the lights."

As I stood there, I could hear the gentle lapping of the water against the pier and hear the wind ruffling the leaves of the trees back in the woods.

The lights flashed on, and we began to walk through the boathouse, side by side. But we only went halfway, because something lying on a wicker settee stopped us. It was Lisbeth. She was naked. And she was dead. Her throat had been slit from beneath her chin down to her collarbone. It wasn't a pretty sight.

I gasped. But before I could release the scream that was welling up within me, Luke said, "Ssshhh!" and quickly walked over to the light switch and snapped it off so the place was in darkness again. I was too terrified and shocked to move until he came back to me and, putting an arm around my shoulders, said quietly, "Come on; I'll take you to your room."

How my feet and legs managed to get me from the boathouse to my room I'll never know, even with Luke's strong arm supporting me. And when we reached the building that was my room, there was another shock awaiting me. The door was wide open, and on the mirror of the door to the bathroom someone had painted a cross, upside down, in fluorescent flame-colored paint so it glowed in the dark.

Luke reached out a hand and snapped on the lights. As far as we could see, the room was the same as it had been when we had left it several hours ago, except that there was a heavy scent of something in the air that smelled like sulphur. I asked Luke if he noticed it. He said, "Yes, it's an incense they use. They make it themselves of various herbs."

"It smells like sulphur."

Luke's face was grim. "It's what they call their Magical Martial Incense of Wrath and Chastisement, and it's made with four parts powdered dragon's blood, four parts dried powdered rue, one part dried ground ginger, one pinch of sulphur and one pinch of magnetized iron filings or powdered lodestone."

"What does it mean?"

"It's a warning. They don't want you here."

"They? Or just Vivienne?" I was beginning to get angry. I wasn't going to be scared off so easily. I tossed my purse on the bed, went to the double-mirrored closet doors and rolled one of them back, took out a pair of navy slacks, removed them from the hanger and put them on the bed. Then I went to the bureau and, opening the middle drawer, took out a black turtle-necked sweater.

Luke asked, "What are you going to do?"

"Go to that coven."

"But you can't! Not now."

I kicked off my pink sandals, ripped off my sheer stockings and got a pair of navy blue sneakers from a shoe rack on the floor of the closet. Standing first on one foot and then the other to put on the sneakers, I asked, "Why not?"

He folded his arms across his chest and looked at me in amazement. "Why not? Are you crazy? You saw Lisbeth, didn't you?"

"Yes, I saw her."

"Well then, do you want to end up like that?"

"No. And I have no intention of doing so."

"I doubt if *she* planned that ending for herself."

Standing on my two sneaker-clad feet, I unzipped the front of my tunic, asking, "Are you going to stay here and watch me change?"

His eyes narrowed and his lips tightened. "No. I have more important things to do." He strode across the room and out of the door. But before he closed it he said, "Lock it."

I did as he told me. Then I looked around the room and made sure the drapes were pulled across the windows and the windows locked. They were. Well, perhaps Lisbeth had done that before — I couldn't finish the thought. Anyway, with the air conditioning, there was no need for the windows to be open.

Quickly I changed my glamorous pants suit of pink to the more somber navy slacks and black sweater. I supposed the more important things Luke had to do were connected with Lisbeth's body, lying on the wicker settee down in the boathouse. Naturally, he would have to notify the police, who would come and swarm all over the place and prevent Vivienne and her friends from holding their coven.

But in this I was wrong. For in a few minutes there was a knock on my door, and when I called, "Who is it?" Luke answered, "It's I. Are you ready?"

I unlocked and opened the door. He had also changed his clothes to dark jeans and a dark sweater. "Did you get them?" I asked.

"Who?"

"Why, the police. You called them about Lisbeth, didn't you?"

"No."

"Why not?"

"Because I didn't want to head off the party in the woods."

"But — ?"

He actually smiled. "Stop arguing and come on, or you'll be late."

I realized there really wasn't any use in arguing. I wanted to see the coven, and if he'd called the police there wouldn't be any coven, so what was there to argue about? I was sure Lisbeth would wait until the coven was over, and then the police could be notified. I supposed we should also notify Doug. The police might want him to come home, because of course there would be an investigation.

This time when we left the room, Luke told me to lock the door, saying, "Not that that will keep anybody out if they want to get in, but it will at least make a little trouble for them."

I said, "All right," and he took the key from the inside of the door, closed it, locked it on the outside and put the key in a pocket of his jeans. Then, taking my arm, he led me along the flower-bordered path for a way, then branched off into what seemed to be wild country. At least there were no paths, and we were suddenly surrounded by trees. The light of the moon was shut off by the thick foliage, and I couldn't see a thing. But we seemed to be going uphill. Luke apparently knew the way and guided me through the darkness. When I asked, "Where are we?" he whispered, "Ssshhh! Voices carry far in the night." When I stumbled over a stone or the root of a tree, he caught me and after that kept a firm arm around my waist. I could hear what I supposed to be small night animals scuttling through the underbrush all around us, but I was afraid to ask what they were. I decided that what I didn't know wouldn't hurt me.

After a few minutes, I began to hear what sounded like voices chanting. I whispered, "Is that they?"

Luke whispered, "Yes. As I told you, they begin their ritual by chanting the Lord's Prayer backwards."

I shivered. "How horrible!"

Gradually I began to see a dim light in the distance. "What's that?" I asked close to Luke's ear.

"Their candles. They burn black candles on the altar."

I remembered the black candles on the mantels in the living room. So they were part of the witches' ritual and not just there for decoration.

The light grew brighter as we neared it. In a moment we came to a sort of clearing in the woods, and I saw we had indeed been going uphill, because the coven was taking place down in a sort of hollow. Luke stopped me and drew me behind the trunk of a tree. Peeking around, I got a good view of the entire scene below us.

In the center of the clearing a white circle had been painted as if with whitewash. Within it was a triangle. At one side, an altar had been built of stones covered with evergreen boughs; and on it, lying on her back, naked except for a black scarf around her waist with the long ends hanging down between her parted legs, was Vivienne. She seemed to be sleeping. Or was she drugged? She wasn't dead, because her breasts were rising and falling as she breathed. Surprising as it seemed, considering her uninteresting face, her body was beautiful. Ariadne's couldn't have been more so. Around her in a semicircle burned the black candles, and there was the same sulphurous scent I had noticed in my bedroom.

Standing around the white circle, completely unclothed, were five men and six women chanting what Luke had told me was the Lord's Prayer backwards. The flickering candles didn't light their faces sufficiently for me to be able to recognize any of them, even if I'd known them. In a way, I was glad of that. I didn't want to discover I knew anyone in that circle. However, to my horror I did recognize Mrs. Davis and — Jason! I gasped. Luke asked, "What?"

I said, "Jason and Mrs. Davis."

He said, "Yes, I know Mrs. Davis."

"She was with Vivienne this afternoon, and she wanted Vivienne to introduce me to their friends, but Vivienne didn't want to."

He said, "That's interesting."

Standing in the center of the circle was a tall black-robed man wearing a black goat's head with large horns. Whether it had originally belonged to a live goat, or whether it was an artificially made contrivance to be slipped over a person's head, I couldn't be sure in the flickering light of the black candles.

Now a goat in itself is not an awesome sight. But when the head of a large black goat, with spirally twisted horns and a long beard, is topping a tall, broad-shouldered man in place of his own head, it can be a frightening thing to see.

Over to one side was a medium-sized black goat tethered to a tree. It looked harmless enough. I was sure it was the same animal I had seen being led off a boat just before dinner.

The chanting stopped, and another kind

of chant began. At this the members of the coven began to dance, backward and forward, into the circle and out again.

The black-robed figure wearing the goat's head stood still, but now he raised his arms as if in a benediction. However, in his right hand he held a long pointed knife with a black handle.

I began to shake and shiver, and I clutched at Luke. He put his arms around me and held me close to him. The contact of his hard warm body was comforting.

After a while the dance and the chanting stopped, and the goat man walked slowly over to the live goat, untied it from the tree and led it to the altar, climbing up onto it and standing so that he and the goat were behind the reclining body of Vivienne. The goat gave a frightened bleat and tried to get away, but the man held him by one horn. Then, slowly and with what looked like great strength, he tilted back the goat's head so that its black-furred throat was exposed.

A wailing chant came from the unclad members of the coven. Then, with a vicious down-thrust, the knife was driven into the goat's throat and blood spurted out, some of it splashing on Vivienne's unconscious face. I opened my mouth to scream, but Luke clamped a hand over my mouth to stop me. Turning to him, I hid my face on his shoulder and stood there shaking. My knees would have given way and let me down if Luke hadn't held me up.

The chanting was continuing, getting louder and louder until it was becoming an hysterical screaming.

I lifted my head, forced to look again. Now the goat was on the ground, dead and gored as if he had been a banderillero's unfortunate horse in a bull fight. The goat man had come down from the altar and was now standing before Vivienne. He still had the knife over the naked body of Vivienne, and drops of blood dripped on her white torso and breasts.

I felt the trees beginning to sway and circle around me, and everything was getting very dark. . . .

That was the last I remembered until I opened my eyes and discovered I was lying on the white velvet sofa in the living room. Someone was sitting in the black satin scoop chair on the other side of the glass table. I blinked, not daring to believe my eyes. It was Doug. When he saw my eyes were open, he smiled. "Hi," he said.

I managed to sit up. When I did I saw my sneakers had dirtied the white velvet at the end of the sofa. Seeing me frown at the spot,

Doug said, "Don't worry about it. It's Scotch-guarded. Just washes off."

I stared at him and ignored the way my heart was acting — jumping, jerking, thumping. I said, "But you *can't* be here! You're in Brussels. I saw you on TV at six o'clock."

"I was in Brussels day before yesterday. They don't always release those news interviews when they actually happen."

That I doubted, but my mind was in no condition to argue. "Where's Luke?" I asked.

Doug said, "I haven't seen him. I just got here. I drove up in a rented car and had one of the inn boats bring me over."

"What time is it?"

He looked at his wrist watch. "Two-thirty."

I glanced around the room. The drapes were drawn over the windows, and several lamps were lit. "Night or morning?" I asked stupidly.

He raised an eyebrow. "Well, I guess you'd call it morning. That is, it's two-thirty A.M." Then he smiled and asked, "What happened to you? Have too much to drink?"

I looked down at myself and saw I was wearing the navy slacks and black sweater I'd put on to go view the coven. "I guess so," I said. "Luke took me to dinner over at the inn on the mainland."

The eyebrows went up again. "Dressed like that?"

I suddenly began to feel afraid. "I changed after we got back, and we went for a walk."

He nodded. The corners of his mouth tightened, and the cleft in his chin deepened. He was wearing a summer seersucker suit, and it was quite rumpled. "I see," he said, and I wondered if he disapproved of me going out with Luke.

I stood up, not too steadily, and said, "I guess I'd better go to bed."

He stood up also. "Which room are you in?" he asked, accompanying me to the door.

His question surprised me, and I felt as if a piece of ice were sliding down my spine. I didn't know what to say, but I had to answer him. "Luke tells me it was your wife's room," I said, feeling very uncomfortable, also somewhat embarrassed.

"Then it is still my wife's room," he said quietly. He opened the door for me, and I said a quick, "Good night."

He nodded and said, "Good night. I'll have Lisbeth bring your breakfast to you about nine. Will that be too early?"

I said, "No. No. That will be fine," and

went out into the night. I couldn't tell him that Lisbeth was dead. I thought he would offer to accompany me to my room merely as a polite gesture, but he didn't, and when he closed the door behind me it was very dark outside. The moon had disappeared, and I felt quite forlorn as I stumbled over to my bedroom all alone.

It wasn't until I reached the building that I realized I didn't have the key. Luke had locked the door and put the key in his pocket, and now I didn't know where he was or which building housed his room. But the lights were on in my room, so maybe, just maybe, he was in there waiting for me. But why, I wondered, had he deposited me in the living room after I had fainted in the woods?

I put my hand on the doorknob, turned it and found the door wasn't locked. I opened it and walked in. Luke wasn't there. But Lisbeth was. She was *in* the bed, under the covers, and the covers were pulled up to her chin so that only her face showed. She looked as if she were asleep, except that her face was as white as the sheet that covered her. I screamed and, turning, ran out of the room, leaving the door wide open. Only I didn't know where to run to. Back to the living room? It was the only place I knew to go. But when I got there, the room was dark. Doug had probably gone to bed. There was a building down the flower-bordered path that had lights in it. That must be his bedroom. Cold with fear and shock, I stumbled to it and knocked on the door. But before my knock was answered, I heard footsteps coming along from the back. In a panic I grabbed the doorknob and opened the door, rushing into the room and slamming the door closed against whoever was coming along the path. Then I stopped and stared. Doug was there, wearing nothing but shorts. He was hanging up a long black robe in a closet at the side of the room, and on the bed was the black goat's head with the long twisted horns. There was no sign of the knife.

I couldn't even scream. I just stood there and stared. Finally I said, "You! *You?* Oh, no, not *you!*"

He finished hanging up the black robe, took out a maroon silk lounging robe, put it on and only then turned to me. "*Now* what's the matter?" he asked, coming over to me.

I backed away from him, but I was only able to go a few steps. Then I bumped into the door which I had slammed so unceremoniously a moment before. "Don't touch me!" I cried, holding up my hands before me to fend him off.

He stopped a few feet away from me. "What on earth is the matter with you, Karen?" he asked. "Are you ill? Do you need a doctor? I've never known you to act like this before. You act as if you were afraid of me."

I didn't answer him. It probably wasn't smart of me to show fear. That would give him an advantage over me.

Finally he said, in his kindest voice, "Come and sit down and tell me about it." He indicated a grouping of chairs before a fireplace that gave one end of the room the feeling of a sitting room. Realizing I was trapped, I did as he suggested. He went to a chest of drawers and opened doors to a liquor cabinet similar to the one in the bedroom I was using. Pouring me some brandy in a beautiful crystal snifter, he came over and handed it to me, saying, "Here, drink this. You're shivering."

I took the snifter in my two hands and sipped some of the brandy. He poured himself a Scotch on the rocks, then sat down in a chair near me, but not close enough to make me feel uncomfortable. Then he said, "Now then, tell me about it."

I decided the truth was the quickest way to get to the bottom of things, so I said, "I saw you wearing that." I nodded toward the goat's head on the bed. "And the black robe tonight."

He kept his eyes on my face, and there was compassion in his eyes. "No, you did not, because I never saw either that fantastic headpiece or the black robe until I came into this room a few minutes ago. The robe is made from one of our fabrics, but that is as much as I know about it."

"But I *saw* you!" I insisted.

"*Where* did you see me?"

"Back in the woods. At the coven. You killed a goat, and then you held the knife dripping with blood over Vivienne. She was lying on an altar, with nothing on but a scarf around her waist and draped down between her legs."

He shook his head; then he smiled sadly. "If I didn't know you so well," he said, "I would think you were on what they call a trip."

I shook my head. "I *saw* you!"

He gulped his drink, still keeping his eyes on my face. "To begin with, Vivienne isn't here, and I don't know what a coven is." He nodded at the brandy snifter I was holding in my two shaking hands. "Drink that!" he ordered me.

I obeyed him, and the liquid warmed me

nicely as it went down my throat and down into my stomach. After a moment I said, "A coven is a group of thirteen people who practice witchcraft — as if you didn't know."

He stared at me for a moment; then he tilted back his head and laughed. "Witches?" he said. "You mean you think I'm a witch?"

"You are apparently the high priest, or whatever they call him, because only *he* is allowed to wear the goat's head."

His laugh quieted down to a chuckle. "My dear Karen," he said, "what did you have to drink tonight?"

"I had two martinis in my room before dinner, then I had a Scotch on the rocks over at the inn, and we had champagne with our dinner."

His chuckle changed to an indulgent smile. "Well, if you don't mind me giving you some advice, I would suggest you go on the wagon. Stick to water, milk, tea, coffee or soft drinks."

The brandy was giving me courage, and some of my panic was leaving me. "I promise you I won't ever tell anybody what I have seen tonight."

He kept smiling. "No, I wouldn't if I were you." Then he added, "Whatever it was, I am sure you will have forgotten it by morning."

"You don't believe me, do you?" I asked. "Or rather, you won't admit the truth."

He reached over and put his empty glass on a table. "Come on now," he said. "I'll take you back to your room."

I put my now empty glass on the table and stood up. "I can't go back to that room," I said.

He stood up and sighed. "I suppose you have a reason?" he asked wearily.

I began to feel breathless as I remembered what the reason was. "Yes, yes, I have," I said. "There's a dead girl in my bed. Lisbeth. They — you — somebody murdered her. Luke and I found her in the boathouse when we came back from dinner. She was lying on one of the wicker settees, and her throat was slit!"

He stared at me. "Then how did she get in your bed?"

"I don't know. Luke and I left her in the boathouse. He was going to call the police after we'd been to see the coven. If we'd called them right away, they'd have come and swarmed all over the island so they wouldn't have been able to have the coven. And Luke and I wanted to see it."

He looked at me in a pitying sort of way.

"Come and show me what's in your room," he said quietly.

I walked toward the door, he opened it, and we went out together. He took my arm and guided me along the flower-bordered path to the room I was occupying. During the few minutes it took us to get there, we didn't talk. A couple of times his hand tightened on my arm in what I supposed he meant to be a reassuring gesture. But instead of reassuring me it frightened me; I wanted to yank my arm away from him, but I didn't dare.

When we reached my room, the door was closed and the lights were out. Still holding my arm, he opened the door and snapped on the lights. There was nothing in or on my bed. It was neatly made up with the pretty white silk coverlet with the signs of the zodiac decorations in gold.

Letting go of my arm, he strode over to the bed, pulled off the coverlet and opened the bed. I held my breath, sure that when the sheets were exposed they would have blood on them. But there wasn't any.

He tossed the covers back and turned to me. "Satisfied?" he asked.

I shook my head. "No, no! She was there. That's why I ran to you. When I came over from the living room, the body was here. I didn't know what to do, and I didn't know where Luke was."

He walked over to me and patted my shoulder. "Well, now you see that there's nothing here, you can go to bed and get some sleep."

"But where is she? Her body, I mean."

His shoulders drooped, and he sighed. "Perhaps we'd better wait until morning to worry about it," he said with forced patience.

"They might have thrown her into the lake."

He began to chew on his under lip. I could see his patience was almost gone. "Well, we can't drag the lake in the middle of the night," he told me. "Tomorrow I'll get into my skin-diving things and go down and look around. I'd rather not bring the police into it if it can be avoided."

"You mean you aren't going to tell the police?"

"Not until I'm sure I have something to tell them."

"But *I'm* telling you! And Luke will tell you. That is, he'll tell you about her being in the boathouse."

He thrust his hands into the pockets of his robe, and from the way the pockets bulged I could tell his hands were clenched into fists.

Then he said, "Well, good night again," strode out of the room and closed the door behind him.

I went over and locked the door, but I had no intention of getting into that bed, not after what I'd seen there a few minutes ago. Neither was I going to put out the lights. I'd just sit in the most comfortable chair and wait for morning. It was already four o'clock. It would be getting light soon.

It wasn't until I'd sat down in the chair that I noticed the upside down cross had been erased from the mirror, where it had been a few hours ago. Who, I wondered, had erased it, and who had taken Lisbeth's body?

Chapter Seven

I must have dozed off in my chair from sheer exhaustion, because the next thing I knew, someone was knocking on the door. With a start, I opened my eyes and discovered it was daylight. It was with difficulty I managed to pull myself awake enough to get out of the chair, go over to the door, unlock and open it.

Luke was standing there. He had a tray with my breakfast. "Good morning," he said, coming into the room and setting the tray down on a table.

I closed the door. I knew I must look awful, but I didn't care. I went around opening the drapes and letting in the sunshine. Immediately the room lost the gruesome atmosphere it had taken on last night and became the bright, beautiful room it had been when I first came into it yesterday afternoon. Was it only yesterday I had arrived? It seemed like a lifetime.

Luke had arranged things on the tray, taking off the domed covers of some of the dishes to disclose bacon and eggs and hot buttered toast. There was also cream and sugar for the coffee that was in a silver pot, and marmalade for the toast. Pulling a chair over to the table, he said, "Sit here."

I sat there. There didn't seem to be any reason to argue it. "Have you eaten yet?" I asked him.

He sat down on a chair near me. "Yes. I ate over in the kitchen. They told me Lisbeth had left and gone home."

"Oh dear!" was all I could say. I noticed he was freshly shaven, his hair was neatly combed, and he had on a wild Hawaiian print short-sleeved sports shirt, open at the throat, and white denim shorts. His arms and legs were deeply tanned.

After a few sips of coffee and some of the bacon and eggs, I asked, "What happened last night?"

He crossed one leg over the other. He had straw espadrilles on his feet. "That's what I want to tell you," he said. "What's the last thing you remember?"

I didn't want to talk about it, but I knew I had to. "Well, the goat man was standing in front of Vivienne, holding the blood-dripping knife over her, and suddenly the trees seemed to start going around and around, and everything began to get black."

He nodded. "You fainted."

I took a bite of toast. "I figured that. And what did *you* do?"

"I caught you as you began to fall, carried you back here and put you on the bed. Then I went down to the boathouse to see about Lisbeth."

"And did you call the police?"

"No. Because just as I entered the boathouse, and before I could snap on the light, something hit me on the back of the head." He felt the back of his head experimentally. "I have a big lump there now." He winced when he touched it. Then he shrugged. "Oh, well — the next thing I knew it was daylight, and I was lying half in and half out of the lake beneath the pier. Why I didn't drown I'll never know."

I stopped eating, because I got a queer feeling in my tummy at the thought of Luke being found drowned. I asked, "Who was it that hit you?"

"If I ever find out, he'll be sorry."

"Then you couldn't see whether Lisbeth was still in the boathouse or not?"

"No, I couldn't. But she must have been."

"Well, she wasn't."

"How do you know?"

"Because along about two o'clock in the morning she was here in my bed."

"But that's impossible. She couldn't have been."

"Well, she was. Are you sure you brought me here and put me on the bed after I fainted, and didn't bring me over to the living room?"

"Of course I'm sure. Why would I take you over to the living room?"

"Because when I came to, I was lying on the white velvet sofa in the living room, and Doug was sitting on the black satin scoop chair on the opposite side of the glass table, looking at me."

He began to smile. "You must have had too much to drink last night."

"That's what he told me." I gave up eating and leaned back in the chair. "I'm beginning to think I don't know anything about anything."

"Where's Doug now?"

"The last I saw of him was when he brought me here, about four this morning."

"What were you doing until four in the morning? It was about twelve-thirty when I carried you here after you'd fainted."

"And you don't know?"

"Of course I don't know. I told you what happened to me."

"Did the goat man kill Vivienne?"

He smiled slightly. "She wasn't there to be killed. She was the virgin. The goat man gets her after the ceremonies."

"But the goat man was Doug!"

He looked at me as if I'd gone completely out of my head. "Oh, come off it! You know Doug is in Brussels. And besides, Doug Randolph would be the last one in the world to violate a virgin, especially Vivienne."

"*That* I wouldn't know. But I saw him hanging the black robe in the closet of his bedroom, and the goat's head was on his bed."

"What were you doing in his bedroom?" his tone was accusing, and I resented it.

"If you'll stop asking me ridiculous questions and discounting everything I say, I'll tell you."

He could see I was angry, so he rolled his eyes heavenward and said, "All right! All right! Go ahead."

I said, "Well, the first thing I knew after everything got black over there in the woods was when I opened my eyes and discovered I was in the living room on the sofa and Doug was sitting watching me. We talked, and I told him how you'd taken me to dinner and then we'd gone to see the coven. But he just thought I'd had too much to drink and didn't take me seriously. So I thought I'd better go to my room, and he let me go alone. I thought that was strange, but I was too groggy to say anything. When I got

143

over here and came in, I found Lisbeth's body in my bed. Not *on* it. *In* it. Naturally, I was shocked and scared. I didn't know where you were, so I ran back to the living room for Doug, but by that time the room was all dark. The only light in any of the buildings was in the one the other side of the living room. So I ran over there and knocked on the door. But before my knock was answered, I heard footsteps coming along the walk from the back. In a panic I tried the doorknob and found the door was unlocked, so I opened it and ran inside and closed the door behind me. Then I realized I was in Doug's bedroom. He was there in his shorts, and he was hanging up the goat man's black robe, and on the bed was the goat's head. To make a long story short, when I accused him of being the goat man, he denied it and asked me why I had burst into his room the way I had. So I told him about Lisbeth's body being in my bed, and he came over here with me to see. But when we got here she was gone, the bed was made up and there wasn't a drop of blood anywhere. By that time he thought I was imagining the whole thing, and he bade me good night and left me. And that was that."

He looked at me thoughtfully. "I wonder who took Lisbeth's body from the boathouse and brought it here?" he said, as if talking to himself.

"*You* didn't?"

He flashed me an angry look. "Of course I didn't. Could it have been Doug?"

"Oh, no!" I cried. "He didn't even know she was dead. The first time we said good night to each other, he told me to sleep late, and he'd have Lisbeth bring me my breakfast about nine."

"That could have been an act."

"Oh, no!" I cried again. "I can't believe Doug is mixed up in any of this, now I've thought it over."

He raised his eyebrows skeptically. "Even though you saw him hanging up the black robe and saw the goat's head on his bed?"

"But he said he'd never seen either of them before until he went to his bedroom and found them there."

"Do you believe that?"

I hesitated. I really hadn't made up my mind yet, but I didn't want him to know that. "Yes and no," I said. "I suppose it's possible, considering the fact that Lisbeth's body was in my bed one minute and gone the next."

He said, "Um." Then, "I wonder where it is now?"

"Perhaps in the lake."

"Quite possible."

"I suggested that to Doug, and he said that this morning he'd go down and look around."

He nodded. "Good idea. He does a lot of skindiving when he's up here."

"Do you skin-dive?"

"Yes. A couple of times this summer, I've gone with him or manned the boat he dives from."

"I don't think I'd like it."

"It's more interesting in the ocean than in a fresh water lake."

"You've skin-dived in the ocean?"

"Yes. When I was in the navy."

"I didn't know that."

He smiled. "There are a lot of things you don't know about me."

"I'm beginning to realize that."

I saw Doug pass one of the windows. He was in his skin-diving suit, carrying the headpiece and flippers. He waved and in another moment knocked on the door. When I let him in, he asked, "Have you seen Luke this morning?"

I stepped aside so he could enter the room. "He's here," I told him. "He brought me my breakfast."

He seemed surprised. "Oh? Well, good

morning, Luke. I'm going to do a bit of exploring. I'll need you to man the boat for me."

Luke stood up. "Okay."

I asked, "Can I come?"

Both men looked at me in surprise; then Doug said, "Are you sure you want to? If we find anything, it won't be pretty."

My stomach contracted. "I know." Then I asked, "Have you seen Vivienne?"

The corners of Doug's mouth tightened, and the cleft in his chin deepened. "No," he said. "The housekeeper told me she and her friends went back to New York sometime during the night. They had cars over on the mainland."

I exchanged a look with Luke. Then I asked, "Wouldn't it be a good idea to call the police and search the entire island?"

Quickly Doug said, "No. Not yet."

But I persisted. "Well, at least shouldn't we go over to the place in the woods where they held the coven and see if — well, if we can find anything?"

"What do you think you'll find?" Doug asked.

"Maybe the body of the goat."

Luke said, "I doubt it. They are not that dumb."

"But I want to see anyway."

Doug questioned Luke. "Perhaps you'd better show me the place." So we left my room, and Luke led us up through the woods to the place where he and I had been the night before. I was still wearing my bedraggled slacks and sweater and soiled sneakers, and my hair and face were a sight, but nobody seemed to care or even notice.

We walked through the woods single file, Luke leading. No one spoke. When we came to the place where Luke and I had stood last night at midnight and looked down at the spot where the altar had been, there was nothing there. Even the white circle and triangle where the witches had danced and chanted was gone. And there was no mutilated goat in sight, no blood and no altar.

I gasped. "But they were there!" I cried. "What have they done with the altar?"

"Dismantled it," Luke told me. "They are too smart to leave any trace of their goings-on."

Without a word, Doug turned and walked back the way he had come, and Luke and I followed him. On the way Doug said, "Karen, you'd better stop off and get yourself cleaned up and some fresh clothes on. We'll wait for you in the boathouse."

So he had noticed. Well, he'd have had to

be blind not to. When I reached my room I took a quick shower, put on clean underclothes, a pair of tan slacks and a thin white roll-neck sweater. I had to admit I felt better; even the sketchy quick attention I gave to my face and hair improved both immeasurably.

When I went down to the boathouse, Luke hailed me from a different boat from the Ariadne. This one was named The Breeze and was sturdier than the Ariadne.

Doug was on board, putting on his flippers, and Luke was waiting on the pier to take me. When I was safely aboard, Luke untied the single line that was holding the boat and pushed it out of the slip; then he jumped on board, went to the bow and did something with the controls. There was a loud roar as he turned on the motor. Then he shifted into reverse and backed out of the boathouse into the lake. Turning the wheel to port, he pushed the gear forward and gunned the throttle. I winced as the engine thundered, jerking the boat forward as the prop hit the water and lifted the bow, shooting a plume of spray. We circled and headed out into the lake.

Turning to Doug, who now had his flippers on and was doing something to his headpiece, Luke asked, "Where do you want to begin to look?"

Doug said, "I don't know. I doubt if they'd throw her into the lake. She could be too easily discovered."

"They almost threw me into the lake," Luke told him.

Doug looked startled. "What do you mean?"

"Last night, after Karen fainted while we were watching the coven and I carried her to her room and put her on the bed, I went to the boathouse to do something about Lisbeth's body. But before I could snap on the lights, someone hit me on the back of the head, and the next thing I knew it was morning and I was lying half in and half out of the lake, underneath the pier."

Doug looked thoughtful. "Who are these *they* you talk about?"

Luke shook his head. "Friends of Vivienne's."

"You don't know any of them?"

"No. Do you know any of her friends?"

"No, I don't." Doug turned to me. "Did you see them last night, Karen?"

"Yes. But I only recognized Vivienne and a friend of hers by the name of Mrs. Carry Davis and Jason. I couldn't get a look at most of their faces. The candlelight was too flickering and too dim."

"Jason?" Doug asked. "You say they were unclothed. Was Jason unclothed, too?"

"Yes."

He raised his eyebrows at that. "I knew he, but I never would have thought —"

"You knew he what?" I asked.

"I knew he had started taking drugs. That was why I let him go. I went down to the garage unexpectedly one time and caught him."

"Oh, dear," I said. "And he seemed so nice."

"He was nice. But he must have gotten in with bad company."

I couldn't help saying, "Vivienne and her friends?"

His brow furrowed. "I don't know — yet."

While we'd been talking, Luke had been circling the boat, not going too far from the island of Sanctuary.

Doug gave his head a shake as if to free him of the thought of Jason and said, "Suppose I go down just off from the boathouse? That's the deepest part of the lake, and I've never gone down there."

Luke said, "Okay," and guided the boat to a point where Doug said, "All right. Here."

Doug put on his headgear, and in addition to his signal line, Luke tied another line around his middle which, they explained to me, he was to cut and fasten to the body if he found it. The very idea gave me the shivers. Then Doug went over the side with a lot of line and dived out of sight.

Luke and I stood there waiting, both too tense to talk. It seemed a long time before Doug signaled that he wanted to surface. Luke informed me that two pulls on the line, then five pulls, meant, "I've finished my work and want to come up."

When Doug surfaced and Luke had helped him up onto the boat, he indicated he wanted to talk. So Luke took off his headpiece for him, and when he saw his face he helped him to a seat, where he sank down as if he didn't have an ounce of strength left. His face was a gray-green beneath his tan, and his lips had no color at all. Luke asked, "What is it? Did you find her?"

Doug shook his head, but he couldn't seem to speak. Finally Luke asked, "Do you want me to go down?"

Doug nodded. He seemed to be in a state of shock, and Luke looked frightened. He went into the cabin, came out with a small glass of brandy and held it to Doug's color-less lips. Then he waited. Doug was shaking now. I put my arms around him and tried to soothe him, but he pushed me away.

Luke said to me, "He must have seen something rather bad."

At last Doug drew in a deep, shuddering breath and, looking straight ahead with eyes that held more horror than I ever want to see in anyone's eyes again, said, "She's down there."

"Lisbeth?" Luke asked.

Doug shook his head. "Ariadne."

"Ariadne?" Luke repeated in a hollow voice. "Are you sure?"

Doug nodded. "She's on a ledge. And there's an anchor tied around her waist."

I gasped.

Luke said, "I'll go down. You've had enough."

From the cabin he got a skin-diving suit, flippers and a headpiece and began putting them on. Doug began to talk then. "She looks just the same as she did the last time I saw her."

"But how can she?" I asked, not realizing how callous my question was.

Luke said, "It's possible. Something about the temperature of the water here and the chemicals in it. It's happened before, I've heard, even after twenty years." He was ready to go down now, and he gripped Doug's shoulder. "Would you rather go back to the house? I can get one of the fellows from the town to come over and help me."

Doug shook his head. "No. I'll be all right. Just get her up." Then more to himself than to us, he said, "She looks so beautiful!"

He stood up then and helped Luke on with his headgear, fastened the line around his waist and helped him over the side. To me he said, "You better go in the cabin. You shouldn't see her when she comes up."

I gritted my teeth and tried not to shiver. "If you can take it, I can," I told him. So we stood side by side at the railing, waiting for the first signal from Luke. It seemed a long time coming. When it did, I helped Doug pull him up, expecting I knew not what. Certainly not the beautifully preserved girl who looked more alive than dead. The only thing that was gruesome was the way her hair was standing out straight from her head as if each hair were wired. Her eyes were open and as blue as they had ever been in life, but they held a look of surprise, as if she couldn't believe what was happening to her.

Luke had her tied to his body so his arms were free. He had cut the anchor off her so he could surface without the added weight.

I would never have believed I could do

such a thing, but I helped Doug pull Luke and his burden over the rail and onto the deck. Then Doug cut the rope that was holding the girl to the man who had brought her up. We laid her gently down on the deck, and Doug knelt down beside her, closed her eyes and smoothed down her hair which, now she was out of the water, went suddenly limp. She was wearing the blue linen suit and the walking shoes Mrs. Watson had said she had had on when she had left the house on East 79th Street a year ago, but the shoulder strap bag was gone. Whether it was on the bottom of the lake or had been lost somewhere else, no one cared at the moment.

Having watched Luke and Doug help each other with the headpieces, I had noticed how it was done, so now I helped Luke out of his. All he said was, "Good girl."

What happened after that was like a bad dream. Luke guided the boat back to the boathouse, the police were called and came, also an undertaker, and then it was all over. Lisbeth had been completely forgotten in the more important happenings of the day.

Chapter Eight

Naturally, Doug tried to get in touch with Vivienne, but her apartment phone was never answered. I wondered if she was still somewhere on the island — alive or dead. But naturally, after the police heard the entire story, which eventually had to come out, they searched every room and every inch of the island. But there was no sign of Vivienne, Carry Davis, Jason or any of the rest of them, whoever they were.

When we got to talking about it, Doug was surprised and annoyed that Vivienne had been up at Sanctuary without his knowing about it.

The only evidence the police found to corroborate Luke's and my story of the coven was the carcass of the goat, which had been hidden in the deepest part of the woods and pushed beneath a thick clump of bushes. There had been no trace of Lisbeth. Professional skin divers were sent for, and they searched the bottom of the lake without any trace of her body.

There was a herb garden in back of the kitchen, but many gourmet cooks liked to raise herbs, so one couldn't very well make anything specific out of that. And the flowerpot over which Vivienne had been saying her verse, ending with, "As I will, so mote it be," was gone.

It was quite evident that Luke and Doug were more than just employer and employee. They were very close friends, and my confusion as to Luke's place in the setup was increased.

The servants, consisting of a middle-aged woman by the name of Naomi Smith, a gardener, an older man named John Daniels and two girls by the names of Sally Shand and Ellen Green who did the cleaning, took care of the rooms and waited on table, were all natives of the village and swore they knew nothing about what went on in the woods or in any of the rooms. Lisbeth had been several years older than they were and had kept to herself; Sally said she had been Vivienne's favorite, that Vivienne had brought her up from the city with her early in the summer. Other than that, no one knew anything about her. All she had ever said about herself was that she was an orphan and didn't have any family. Whether or not she was one of Vivienne's coven, no one knew, or why she had been killed. Everybody said she was a nice girl.

Naturally, the discovery of Ariadne's body raked up the entire story from the day she had disappeared, a year before. A new investigation was started, and the papers made the most of it. Jason was located and questioned, but he swore he knew nothing. He also swore he was not one of the coven the night Luke and I had seen it. And how could it be proved? When asked why he had left Mr. Randolph's employ, he said he'd been discharged without any explanation, that Mr. Randolph had given him six months' salary in lieu of notice. When Doug was questioned about that, instead of telling the truth about it, for Jason's sake, he said it was because the board of directors of Amalgamated Fabrics had been worried about his safety after the strange disappearance of Ariadne and wanted him to have a man who was not only a chauffeur but who could act as a bodyguard as well. It was then that it came out that Luke was an F.B.I. man and had been put on the case not only to guard Doug but to further the investigation of Ariadne's disappearance as well.

Doug didn't want to take Ariadne's body back to the city, but instead had her buried in a small cemetery on the mainland.

Up to the time of the funeral, Vivienne had not been located. Finally the city police were sent to her apartment and found she hadn't been there for quite some time. The neighbors knew nothing about her, nor did the superintendent of the building.

We thought the publicity given the discovery of Ariadne's body would bring Rudy at least to the funeral. But there was no word from him. He didn't even send flowers. His office said they did not know where he was. The last they had heard from him, he had been in Australia with his new client.

It was the evening after the funeral that a very eerie thing happened. Doug, Luke and I were sitting in the living room having an after-dinner drink. It was about ten o'clock when suddenly all the lights went out and the white grand piano at the end of the room began to play a Chopin Etude. It was the Revolutionary Etude, which in itself is very dramatic and in this instance seemed even more so.

Doug said, "My God!"

Luke said, "What the — ?"

And I said a gasping, "Oh!"

Then for several minutes we just sat there listening. The moon was shining in the window beside the piano, because no one had pulled the drapes, and we could see the white and black keys were moving as if fingers were playing upon them. But there was no one on the white chair with the tufted seat which was before the instrument. Finally I asked, "It's a pianola?"

Doug said, "No!"

"It's a trick, that's for sure," Luke said.

Doug said, "It's she. It sounds just like her."

"Don't be silly!" Luke snapped. "It's a record hidden somewhere."

"But a record wouldn't move the piano keys," Doug argued. His voice trembled, and my heart went out to him, but I dared not offer sympathy.

Finally Luke got up, saying, "This is ridiculous!" and went over to the light switch. But when he touched it, nothing happened. "A fuse must have blown," he said. Just then the piano began to play louder and faster. Luke tried a couple of lamps, but they wouldn't light, either, and by now the moon had gone under a cloud so I couldn't see either of my companions.

Doug asked, "Got a match? Light the black candles on the mantelpiece." But I couldn't resist crying out, "Oh no!" Just then the piano stopped playing with a final descending of chords and a loud crash. I heard the sound of a door closing, the light went on — and I was in the room all alone.

Luke and Doug were gone!

I screamed, "Doug! Luke!" But no one answered me. I got up and went over to the piano. I do not believe in ghosts, and I knew Ariadne was dead and buried, but something had played that piano. I sat down on the chair and ran my fingers over the keys. They played quite naturally. I knew the Revolutionary Étude by heart myself. It had been one of my assignments in college, and I had had to practice it every day for an entire semester. I began to play it, wondering what would happen. Nothing did until I had gotten halfway though. Then the piano keys suddenly began to play by themselves again, faster than my fingers could go. I snatched my hands away from the keyboard, startled and almost paralyzed with fright. What was this thing that gave a piano a life of its own? I should have gotten up and left the instrument, but I couldn't. I just sat there, watching the keys playing by themselves.

When the door opened and Doug and Luke came in, I turned. "Get away from there!" Doug ordered me.

I got up and left the piano, which was finishing the étude all by itself, the descending chords ending with the final clash. "Where did you go?" I asked him.

Luke answered, "We've been trying to find the person who is doing that," nodding toward the piano.

"Then you think it's a *live* person?"

"Of course. You don't believe in ghosts, do you?"

"No. No."

Doug went over to the piano and began looking underneath it and inside where the strings were. "It could be done electronically," he said thoughtfully. "But someone must be manipulating it from somewhere."

Finding nothing, he said, "Well, I suppose we might as well go to bed. Tomorrow is another day, and I have to get back to the city." He turned to me. "Do you want to come back with me?" he asked.

I said, "Oh yes! I don't want to stay here."

He came over to me and patted my shoulder. "Not much of a vacation for you, I'm afraid."

I managed a weak smile. "That's all right. It's not your fault."

"Well, it's *somebody's* fault!" Luke said. "And I'd like to find out whose."

Doug turned to him. "When did you get here?" he asked.

"A couple of days before Karen. You said you wanted me to go over the boats while you were away."

162

Doug said, "Yes, that's right." Then he asked, "Was Vivienne here when you got here?"

Luke said, "Yes she was. And so was her friend Mrs. Davis."

I couldn't help saying, "I wonder where Vivienne is now."

"I'd like to know that myself," Doug said. He went over to the piano and closed it, pulling the lid over the keys and letting down the gracefully curved top. The strings gave a sound that was almost like a grunt of protest, and Doug started, gave it a questioning look, then turned and walked away from it. Coming over to me, he took my arm. "Come on. I'll see you to your room," he said gently. Then to Luke, "I'll be right back."

Luke said, "Okay. Good night, Karen."

I said, "Good night, Luke," feeling as if I were going into I knew not what. But why should I feel apprehensive, when all I was going to do was walk a few yards on a flower-bordered path to my room in the company of the man I loved? Or did I love him — now? Had the happenings of the last few days shown him to be just an ordinary man instead of the exalted being I had been thinking he was? Was it fair to expect any man to be an exalted being?

Walking beside me, my arm in a firm grip

to keep me from stumbling, he said, "I've been thinking, Karen, perhaps you'd rather not stay with Amalgamated Fabrics when your vacation is over."

"Not stay with Amalgamated Fabrics?" I cried, my voice high-pitched and childish-sounding. "Why not?"

"Well, working for me certainly isn't — may not be the best thing for you."

"What else would I do?"

His hand on my arm tightened, and suddenly I was aware of the night sounds of the country: the chorus of night insects which, when you actually listened to them, were sharp and strident; the occasional hoot of a night owl in the distance, which was a lonely and depressing sound; and closer, the gentle swish of the lake water against the shore of the island. This last made me shiver involuntarily, because it reminded me of the way Ariadne looked when Luke brought her up from the depths of that very lake.

Doug let go of my arm and put his arm around my shoulders. "You're cold," he said gently.

I said, "I guess it's just nerves."

"And no wonder," he said, giving me a little hug. "You've been through a lot the past few days."

"So have you."

He didn't answer right away, but I could feel his body tense. After a moment he said, "When it's all over — and I hope it is now — would you consider marrying me?"

I stopped and caught my breath. "Oh! I don't know," I gasped.

He took his protective arm from my shoulders and let me walk a couple of steps ahead of him. "I'm sorry," he said behind me. "I shouldn't have said that. It's too soon. Forgive me."

I heard a scuffling sound behind me and turned to see what he was doing, but he was gone. I was there on the flower-bordered path — alone. I cried, "Doug! Where are you?" There was no answer.

I was on the verge of panic. He couldn't have just disappeared. There was no place for him to disappear; no bushes or trees behind which he could hide. But the moon was still under a cloud, and it was dark. I couldn't see my hand before my face. I looked back at the building that housed the living room. It was lighted the way it had been when we had left it, and I knew Luke was there, waiting for Doug to return. I began to run back to the building, not wanting to continue on to my room all alone.

When I reached the door to the living

room, I opened it and cried, "Luke!" Then I screamed. Standing over by the white concert grand piano, which was now silent and closed, the way Doug had left it, was the goat man, complete with long black robe and the fantastic goat's head with the twisted horns.

He turned and looked at me, then raised his hands and began to lift the goat's head from his own. But I did not see whose face was being disclosed to me. I couldn't bear it. Suddenly I felt as if every drop of blood were draining out of my body, and darkness closed in around me.

Chapter Nine

The first thing I became conscious of was the fact that I was cold. And I was lying on something hard. Gradually the sound of chanting voices came to my ears.

I opened my eyes and thought my heart was going to beat its way right out of my chest. Standing over me, with a long knife dripping blood down on my bare torso, was the goat man.

Suddenly I realized I was in the same position Vivienne had been the night Luke and I had seen her through the trees, in the same state of undress and, to my fast accumulating horror, lying on a similar altar, surrounded by flickering black candles.

I screamed and sat up, but the goat man was too close to me. I couldn't get to my feet. Behind him I could see naked people dancing, as they chanted what I now recognized was the Lord's Prayer backward. I cried, "Oh no! Please! Let me go!" But the goat man tossed away the bloody knife and lifted me up in his arms. "Shut up!" he said sharply. The sound of his voice was muffled as it came through the fantastic goat's head he was wearing, and I could not have recognized it even if I'd known who was wearing it.

Pushing past the naked dancers, he strode out of the circle and into the woods. "Please let me go!" I cried, struggling frantically in his arms. "Whoever you are, let me go!"

But he just held me tighter, and the beard of the goat's head tickled my bare, blood-smeared torso.

I've never been very religious, although my brother and I were always taken to Sunday School when we were small, and my mother and father usually went to church services Sundays, but now I began to pray. "Please God, save me from this monster and this evil, whatever it is!" As if in answer to my prayer, I saw we were nearing the complex of houses known as the Randolph place. "Where are you taking me?" I asked the goat man, a sob in my voice.

"Where you'll be safe," he told me.

"Safe? With *you?*" I tried to wrench out of his arms but only succeeded in loosening the scarf that was my only protection in the way of clothing.

I started pounding on his chest with my clenched fists. "Whoever you are, Doug, Luke, whoever, let me go!"

He didn't seem to notice the scarf falling

as he was carrying me into my room, nor did he pay any attention to my pounding fists. He strode across the room and dropped me on the bed. Then he took the ruffle of the bedspread with the signs of the zodiac decorating it and covered me with it. I grabbed at it and held it close to me. I was shivering, not only from the coolness of the night but also from a nervous chill.

Standing beside the bed, the goat man lifted the goat's head from his own. Watching him, too frightened to move, I saw my rescuer was Rudy. Rescuer?

"*You?*" I cried.

He smiled, and my blood ran even colder than it had been doing up to that moment.

He said, "Yes, *me*. Sorry if you expected Luke or Doug."

I couldn't answer him, because I didn't know whom I had expected. I had thought the goat man in the living room was Luke, but maybe he hadn't been.

Rudy began to take off the long robe, and I saw that underneath he just had on a pair of shorts and an undershirt.

"What are you going to do?" I asked in a strangled voice. He pulled the undershirt up over his head, leaving his torso bare, "What do *you* think?" he asked me with a grin that was nothing short of diabolical. Then he added, "It's better than having your throat slit by one of the others."

I moved then. Rolling to the other side of the bed, I got to my feet and ran for the door which, with me in his arms, he'd been unable to close when he carried me into the room. Fear seemed to give wings to my feet, and I managed to reach the door before he could intercept me. I grabbed up the scarf that was just inside the door.

With a trembling hand, I wrenched open the screen door, which was on a spring, and held the scarf up in front of me to cover my nakedness. But my efforts gained me nothing, because just as I stepped out into the night I was picked up bodily by another goat man, who started to run with me toward the boat house. I screamed then, stupidly enough. Rudy at least I knew, but this new goat man was an unknown quantity. But my screaming didn't do me any good, because the goat man didn't pay any attention to it.

Back in the room I had just left, I could hear furniture overturning and glass breaking, but I couldn't imagine why.

This new goat man was nearing the boathouse now, and as he entered it, with me fighting frantically in his arms, he snapped on the light with an elbow. The place was empty, and he hurried through it and down to the launch with the name Ariadne painted on its prow, the one I had arrived on. Jumping on board, he almost threw me into the cabin just as another man, who I saw was Luke, ran through the boathouse and, jumping on board, started the launch with a noise that rent the stillness of the night.

In the cabin, I sank down on a folding chair, still clutching at the scarf. The new goat man came in, went to a locker at the end of the cabin and took out a pair of dungarees and a sweater. Throwing them at me, he said through the goat's head, "Put them on."

Gladly I did as he ordered, even though I knew they would be many sizes too large for me.

The launch was backed out into the lake now, and was turning and heading for the mainland.

My hands were trembling so I had difficulty getting into the dungarees and sweater. But finally I managed to get them on, folded up the trouser legs and rolled up the sweater sleeves so I could have some freedom of movement.

While I had been doing that, the goat man had taken off the goat's head and the long black robe. Looking at him, I saw he was Doug. "Oh, Doug!" I cried and threw myself into his arms.

He held me close for a moment, saying, "There, there, you're safe now." With a sigh, I laid my head upon his shoulder. From the deck Luke called, "Hey, Doug, come out here. I think they're following us."

Both Doug and I ran out on deck and looked back at the boathouse, which was still brightly lighted and from which another launch was backing out into the lake.

"Can they overtake us in that?" Luke asked.

Doug said, "No. This is the fastest boat we have. Give it all it can stand, and we'll make the mainland far enough ahead of them to get into the inn and call the police."

Luke said, "Right-o," and the launch seemed to leap forward like something alive.

Doug pulled me down on the side seat and put an arm around me, holding me close to him. "I'm still scared," I said tremulously.

Hugging me even closer, he said, "Don't be. It's all over now, and you're safe. We'll be in the city by morning. The car is in the inn garage."

The moon had finally slid from beneath the cloud, and I could see Luke's back as he stood in the prow of the boat, guiding it with his strong, sun-browned hands. I thought his back and his entire body looked rigid, not relaxed the way he usually was. What had happened back in the room? How had he and Doug known I needed rescuing?

The launch was cutting though the water at such great speed that spray was flying up and wetting Doug and me quite thoroughly. Luke was protected by a glass windshield, but it was wet to the point of being difficult to see through it.

Luke asked, "Are they gaining on us?"

Doug leaned over the rail and looked back. "No, I don't think so."

I asked, "What are you going to tell the police? They really haven't done anything criminal."

Doug said, "Only killed my wife and Lisbeth."

"But how can you prove that?"

He didn't answer for a moment, then said, "I don't suppose I can. But I should be able to prove they have drugs in their possession. I'd be willing to bet that that is at the bottom of this whole thing. I've warned the police to look for them."

Luke said, "Doug, witchcraft hasn't anything to do with drugs. There's more to it than that."

Doug said, "Oh, witchcraft! The whole idea is ridiculous."

Luke said, "Maybe so. But in some way or other it was responsible for Ariadne's death."

"I don't believe it. But I'll find out. And when I do —"

"If you don't get yourself killed first," Luke said succinctly.

I clutched at Doug. "Oh do be careful," I begged. The bells weren't actually ringing, but they were on the verge of it.

"They won't kill me," he assured me. "Don't worry."

I had to ask, "Do you think Ariadne was part of the happenings?"

Doug said, "No, of course not."

Quietly Luke said, "That's where you're wrong, Doug. Didn't you know that both Ariadne and Vivienne were witches?"

Explosively Doug said, "You're crazy!"

"I'm sorry, Doug," Luke said. "You had to know sometime."

We were nearing the pier in front of the inn now. I had another question I wanted Doug to answer before it was too late to ask it. "Doug, why did you come back from Brussels so suddenly?"

"Luke telephoned me. He knew Vivienne wasn't supposed to be here, and he didn't think it was safe for you to be here at the same time she was."

"Luke?" I cried. I looked at Luke accusingly, but he just grinned. "I didn't think he'd get here so quickly."

"But you let me think —"

"I know what I let you think. It was the best way."

The launch zoomed up beside the pier, and the motor stopped. The stop had been so sudden the boat rocked precariously from side to side so I couldn't get to my feet. Luke turned and took hold of me, and with him pulling me and Doug giving me a shove from the back, I managed to get out onto the pier. But I felt tottery and had to lean against Luke. He held me against his strong body until Doug was on the pier beside me. Then Doug put a steadying arm around me, and the three of us hurried along the pier, across the road and into the inn. With our own motor silent, we could hear the motor of the pursuing boat, which seemed to be coming nearer with a frightening speed.

When we were safely in the foyer of the inn, with other people milling about and the lights brightly shining, Doug turned me over to Luke and said, "I'll call the police from that booth downstairs in the grill."

Luke stood holding my arm, and I could

feel the tension in him. I asked shakily, "They can't hurt us here?"

Luke said, "No." I could feel a barrier between us. The easy camaraderie we had had the night when we had dined here at the inn and then gone to the movies was gone. Foolishly I thought, It's gone with the wind.

Doug came upstairs and said, "They are coming right away."

There was a lounge at the side of the lobby, where there were comfortable-looking sofas and chintz-upholstered wing chairs. I asked, "Can't we go in there and sit down?" My knees were protesting about holding me up or I wouldn't have asked.

But Doug said, "No. We aren't going to sit here and wait for them." Then to Luke, "Is the car all ready?"

Luke said, "Yes. There's a back door we can go out to get to the garage. Maybe we'd all better go together."

So, with Doug on one side of me and Luke on the other, we went through the lobby and out a back door. We could still hear the motor of the other boat as we went into the dimly lighted garage. The cadillac was parked at the back, and we almost ran over to it. The thought flashed through my mind that it would seem strange to be sitting on the back seat of the car beside Doug, with Luke sitting up front doing the driving, like a chauffeur. Somehow I could no longer think of Luke as a chauffeur. But Doug, bless him, opened the front door and said to me, "Hop in. We can all sit in the front seat."

Luke had gone around to get in the driver's seat, and in less time than it takes to tell, the big black car was rolling out of the garage with me sitting between Luke and Doug.

The driveway from the garage went out to the public road at the far end of the inn toward the town, past the point where it could be seen from the pier. So even though we could hear the pursuing boat stop its motor with explosive putts that meant it had arrived at the pier, we couldn't see it by looking back, nor could they see us. A low siren wail told us the police had arrived. They whizzed past us without noticing who we were. Doug said, "Well, we made it." Luke, tightening his lips, put on speed, and the big black car seemed to fly over the road rather than proceed on wheels. Luke said, "We can get on the main road down here a way."

Suddenly I asked, "Why are we running away if we have the police to protect us?"

Luke said, "That's a good question."

Doug said, "I've got to get something more specific before I can actually accuse them. In the meantime, I'm afraid for Karen."

I asked, "Who is *them?*"

Doug said, "Well, you saw Rudy. And you say you saw Jason that other night."

"Yes." I shivered at the thought of both of them.

"And you saw Vivienne."

"But we don't know where *she* is."

From behind us her voice said, "You do now. I'm right here."

She must have been hiding on the floor in the back of the car. In our hurry, what with the bad lighting in the garage, we hadn't noticed her.

Doug turned around, and I could feel him start. Reaching behind my back and over my head, he made a grab for something, saying explosively, "Put that thing down!"

Vivienne laughed. "Oh, no, my dear brother-in-law. I've got you just where I want you at last, and I'm not going to give an inch."

Glancing in the rear-view mirror, Luke snapped, "Don't be a fool, Vivienne. You can't get away with anything more."

"Can't I? We'll see. Pull over to the side of the road and stop."

"Like fun I will," Luke told her.

Turning my head slightly, I saw the barrel of a pistol pressed against the back of Luke's neck. My heart nearly jumped out of my body, and without a moment's hesitation I turned and grabbed the barrel of the pistol and pushed it upwards. It went off, but the bullet went out the open window just over Luke's head and struck a tree. In an instant Doug had turned, gotten on his knees on the front seat and grabbed Vivienne's shoulders, shaking them as hard as he could. Taken by surprise, she dropped the gun from her hand, and it fell over my shoulder and into my lap. Luke, guiding the car to the side of the road, stopped it and in a fraction of a second was out of the door beside him and in the back door, grabbing Vivienne around the waist, pulling her out of Doug's grasp and throwing her onto the back seat, where she lay with the breath knocked out of her, too surprised to move.

Before she could stir, Doug was in the back from his side of the car, and between them he and Luke had her pinioned so she was helpless.

"Now!" said Doug. "Talk!"

She didn't answer him.

Luke said, "You might as well. We know everything anyway." Which, I knew, wasn't strictly true.

Doug said, "You know we found Ariadne."

Still she didn't speak.

"And we know all about the covens and all the rest of it."

Her silence continued.

"We don't know yet who killed Lisbeth or Ariadne. But we'll find out."

To this Vivienne said a derisive, "Ha!"

Doug slapped her face.

I flinched at that, even though I realized she deserved it. Still, I wished he hadn't.

Doug asked Luke, "Is there any rope in the trunk of the car?"

Luke said, "Yes. Can you hold her while I get it?"

"Her and three more like her," Doug said, his teeth clenched.

And he did hold her, in spite of the way she fought him while Luke was getting the rope. When they had her hands and feet tied, Doug said, "I guess we'd better take her back to the inn. The police must still be there. They haven't passed us on the way back to the village."

Luke said, "All right." He came and got into the front seat where I was sitting, feeling bewildered and useless. The gun was still in my lap. I hadn't dared touch it. He saw it, took it and put it into his pocket. "I don't think you want this

180

thing," he said with a slight smile.

I said, "No."

He turned the car around and headed back to the inn. Vivienne, now quiet on the back seat, with Doug guarding her, said, "Are *you* going to get a surprise when you get back there!"

No one answered her, so she said, "If you're smart, you'll mind your own business."

Doug said, "What goes on in Sanctuary *is* my own business."

"You are very smug, my dear brother-in-law," she said derisively. "But what you don't know is that Ariadne never was in love with you. She only married you because you had money, and she needed money to further her career."

Doug was silent for a moment. Then he said, "I don't believe that."

"That's because you're stupid. She and Rudy had had a thing going for a long time. Didn't you know?"

Doug said, "No, I didn't, and I don't believe it."

"Suit yourself."

We were in sight of the inn now, and the police car was parked out front.

Luke asked, "Where do you want me to stop?"

Doug said, "In front. Behind the police car."

"What are you going to do with the excess baggage?" Luke asked, meaning Vivienne.

Doug thought a moment before saying, "I guess we'll have to carry her in with us. We can't leave her in the car."

Luke stopped behind the police car, where roof lights were lit and revolving rhythmically. Getting out of the front seat, he helped Doug lift the tied-up Vivienne from the car, he taking her feet and Doug lifting her beneath the arms. She let them carry her without trying to fight them. I asked, "Shall I come with you?" and Doug called over his shoulder, "Yes. You can't stay out here all alone." So I got out of the car and followed them up the steps and into the foyer of the inn, feeling very apprehensive.

The woman behind the desk looked surprised but, quickly sizing up the situation, said, "They're in the lounge." Glancing into the room where I had wanted to sit and rest a short while ago, I saw that Rudy and one policeman were sitting on a sofa, and another policeman was sitting in a chair facing them. They seemed to be chatting amicably and even laughing.

Doug and Luke marched into the room

and dropped Vivienne down onto another sofa not far from the one Rudy was sitting on. The three men looked up in surprise, and the policeman who was sitting in the chair jumped up and went over to them. "What's this?" he asked when he saw Vivienne was tied up.

Doug said, "Another one of the gang. She was hiding in the back of my car and tried to hold us up at gun point."

Rudy got up and sauntered over. I noticed he had an ugly-looking scratch on one cheek, and his eyes were puffed and bruised. His nose didn't look too good, either. He had on a pair of dungarees and a T-shirt which he could have found in a locker on the launch in which he had come over from the island. From the looks of them, they could belong to Doug. They were a couple of sizes too large for him. He hadn't had time to go from my room to get something of his own and get to the launch in which he'd followed us; he had been too close behind us. To Vivienne he said, "Where have *you* been?"

She was lying on her back on the sofa, and I almost felt sorry for her, she looked so helpless and undignified. For the first time I noticed she had on slacks and a sweater, both light blue. "That's *my* business!" she told Rudy.

"Don't talk to *me* that way," he told her. "You're in no position to."

The policeman who had been sitting on the sofa beside him came over and began talking to Doug. He said, "Mr. Vanderhoff tells us the gang you were expecting took one of the other boats and has gone to the other end of the lake." I realized that Rudy was probably known to them from previous summers when he had been up there as a guest of Ariadne.

Doug's face tightened. "Mr. Vanderhoff is one of them," he said tersely. "I want you to arrest him here and now!"

The two policemen looked surprised. Finally the first one asked, "On what charge, Mr. Randolph?"

Doug said, "Assault and attempted rape — for a start. We'll get to the other charges later."

Still the policeman hesitated. "Whom did he assault?" he asked.

"This young lady," Doug told him, pointing to me.

The policeman turned to me. "Is this true?" he asked me.

"Er — yes, yes, it is," I said hesitantly.

"You don't seem to be very positive about it," the policeman said.

Luke was watching me, and Doug seemed

surprised at my hesitancy. "Yes, he did," I said more positively. "Doug — er — Mr. Randolph rescued me just in time." I felt silly saying it, even though it was true.

The policeman looked at Rudy. "Is he the one who messed up your face?"

Rudy began to look uneasy. "No. Luke did that."

"Luke?" the policeman asked.

"I did," Luke told him. And for the first time I noticed Luke's face looked a bit scratched, too, and his lip was cut and had dried blood on it.

The policeman asked, "And who are you?"

"I'm the chauffeur," Luke told him.

The policeman appeared skeptical. "The chauffeur?" he questioned. "You're not the one who was up here last summer."

Doug said, "No, that was Jason. Luke has been with me for about ten months."

The policeman said, "Well, you're sure you want Miss Westmore and Mr. Vanderhoff arrested?"

Doug said, "Very definitely."

When the policeman spoke of them by their names, names that were part of our daily life — mine and Doug's and even Luke's — it just didn't seem real. But it was very real, and I had to face it.

The policeman took a pair of handcuffs from his pocket, and turning to Rudy, said, "I'm sorry, Mr. Vanderhoff, but I'll have to put these on you. I'll take you in the police car with me." He turned to the other policeman. "And Officer Greely will go in Mr. Randolph's car with Miss Westmore."

Vivienne made a movement of protest on the sofa. "This is ridiculous!" she said petulantly.

Officer Greely began to untie her. "We'd better free you so you can walk out to the car," he said. "We don't want to get the guests here at the inn too upset."

She didn't answer him but held out her hands so he could get at the knots. The other policeman untied the knots in the ropes that were tied around her ankles.

When she was free, she sat up on the sofa and rubbed her wrists and ankles. "You'll be sorry for this, Douglas," she said without looking at him.

"I doubt it," he told her.

We left the inn in a group. Officer Greely took hold of Rudy's arm, which the other policeman, whose name we hadn't heard yet, took hold of Vivienne.

Rudy and Officer Greely got into the police car and zoomed off, and the rest of us got into the cadillac; Luke, Doug and I in the front seat and the policeman and Vivienne in the back. The only words that were spoken as Luke followed the police car were those the policeman addressed to Vivienne: "I'm sorry about your sister. She was a nice lady."

Vivienne said, "Thank you."

When we reached the police station a cluster of people seemed to appear from nowhere and stood watching us go into the building.

Inside, Doug made his charges to the sergeant at the desk, and I had to back him up, as did Luke. The sergeant looked unhappy about the whole thing and asked Vivienne and Rudy if they wanted to make a phone call. They both said no and refused to try to raise bail, so they were booked and led away to be locked up until their formal arraignment in the morning. Which meant we'd have to stay over.

As we left the police station, Doug asked me, "Would you rather get a room at the inn for the night than come back to Sanctuary?"

I thought quickly. "Yes, I think I would. If you don't mind?"

"Not at all."

What we didn't know was that Vivienne and Rudy would be thoroughly questioned by the police during the night and that, faced with the uncompromising determination of the law to get to the bottom of the whole thing, they would both break down and tell the truth about all the strange happenings on Sanctuary and the demise of Ariadne and Lisbeth. It was like a horror movie, and when we learned the truth about everything, Doug and I were brought closer together in some ways and pushed farther apart in others.

Chapter Ten

Gradually I reconstructed the past.

It seemed that Ariadne and Vivienne, who were originally Helen and Anna Westmore, first became interested in witchcraft after their parents died and they moved into the Chelsea apartment. Mrs. Carry Davis had an apartment on the same floor with them, and it was she who converted them to the cult, if you can call it that.

Anna became interested in it first and Helen later. By the time Helen met and married Douglas Randolph, she had changed her name to Ariadne, both in her personal and her professional life. It seemed to be a turning point for her; it wasn't until after she became Ariadne that she gained success as a pianist. It was also before she met and married Doug that she met Rudy, who was at that time just a struggling public relations man. He was one of Mrs. Davis' friends whom she had converted to witchcraft.

But concerts at Town Hall cost money, and the Westmore girls, although they were able to live comfortably on the income left them by their parents, did not have the kind of money necessary to give concerts there. So after Ariadne met Doug at a party one evening and a couple of months later he asked her to marry him, Rudy advised her to do so.

For a while she hesitated. She liked Doug, but the divine spark wasn't there. However, after Rudy had carefully pointed out how Doug's money could further her career, not only by financing her concerts, but also by providing the publicity necessary to launch any artist, no matter how talented, she succumbed and told Doug she would marry him.

What she didn't know was that Rudy had a double purpose in wanting her to marry for money. One: he sincerely believed in her talent. And two: he wanted to be her agent, and in that capacity he wanted to assure himself of a fee that would enable him to live in a manner to which he had never been accustomed, having grown up on the West Side of the city with a father who was a longshoreman and a mother who was a waitress.

And so Ariadne, Helen Westmore, became Mrs. Douglas Randolph, wife of the president of Amalgamated Fabrics, Inc.

To give the devil his due, Ariadne did everything in her power to be a good wife. But her music always came first. And after the first couple of years, she found that her husband's business always came first with him, even though he was genuinely in love with his wife. In such a situation it was only too easy for an unscrupulous man like Rudy to wedge himself in, and for a jealous girl like Vivienne to influence her sister to give more and more of her time to the art of witchcraft — and not only her time but her money as well.

Rudy, although not actually won over to witchcraft, saw in it another way to manipulate Ariadne. And so the evil built up around her in a way she was too naïve to notice.

The fact that she never complained about Doug leaving her alone so often for business dinners and business trips lulled him into a false sense of security as far as the love of his wife was concerned. He was only too glad that she had her music to keep her occupied, so that he could immerse himself in his business affairs without the usual recriminations with which most wives would have made his life miserable.

And so the thing built up until the time when Ariadne disappeared — a happening which Doug could not understand, nor could the police.

It was Vivienne who had been responsible

for Sanctuary becoming a haven for her witch friends. I say *her* friends, because Ariadne had never really become converted to their ways, and it was because of this that she had had the bad fortune of ending up at the bottom of the lake.

The day of her disappearance had been August 1st, and Vivienne and her coven had planned a ceremony on the island for that evening. But Ariadne had refused to join them because of the engagement she and Doug had with their friends for that very evening. Vivienne had pleaded and argued with her, but Ariadne was adamant. She said they were welcome to go up to the island if they wanted to, but she had enough feeling for her husband to want to please him in any way she could, and she knew he liked her to spend an occasional evening with him and some of their friends.

But Vivienne did not like to be crossed and made up her mind she was going to get her sister up to the island to attend the coven, by fair means or foul.

In the all-night questioning by the police in the little station house in Pinecrest, the story all came out.

It had been Vivienne who had telephoned Ariadne that fateful morning in August, asking her sister to meet her in a small store down on lower Second Avenue, where witches' chalices, jewelry and working tools were sold. She needed Ariadne to pay for the purchases she intended to make, and Ariadne was always ready to help her witch friends with money, even if she didn't go along with all their beliefs. So she agreed to meet her sister in the store indicated. But when she arrived she found Mrs. Davis was there with Vivienne, and Vivienne had her car at the curb to transport the articles that were being bought in the dingy shop.

When they finished shopping, Vivienne told Ariadne they would drive her uptown in time for her to be home for lunch, as long as she wouldn't go up to Sanctuary with them. But when she got into the car, Mrs. Davis gave her a shot of something that knocked her out for several hours. When she came to, she was in her room on the island, with Vivienne and Mrs. Davis sitting beside her.

When she saw where she was, she was furious and tried to get off the bed and run out of the room. But Mrs. Davis was too quick for her, caught her and gave her another injection. Unfortunately, she gave her too much of whatever the drug was, and Ariadne died a few minutes after it had been administered.

Mrs. Davis and Vivienne were terrified when they realized what they had done and didn't know what to do. They couldn't let anyone know Ariadne was dead, but neither could they return to the city and leave her body in the room on the island of Sanctuary.

There was only one thing to do: dispose of the body. But how? The lake, of course. So they waited until after dark, and then they carried the body down to the lake. In the boathouse, they found an old anchor, and to assure themselves that the body would not later rise to the surface and float so it would eventually be found, they tied the anchor around her waist.

What they didn't know was that where they rolled the body in there was a ledge part way down, and Ariadne would be caught and held on this ledge until the day Doug went down in his skindiving outfit looking for Lisbeth and instead found the body of his wife.

Vivienne and Mrs. Davis had rented a boat in Pinecrest to get from the mainland to the island, saying that Ariadne was ill and that was the reason they had to carry her from the car to the boat. They had paid the elderly man from whom they had rented the boat well, threatening him with dire consequences if he ever told anyone about it. That was the reason he had not come forward and told what he knew when the search was started for Ariadne.

As a matter of fact, the search did not extend to Sanctuary at that time because no one had thought she would go up there alone. She never went alone, always having either Doug or Vivienne with her when she went, and often Rudy.

Needless to say, Vivienne and Mrs. Davis were terrified by what they had done. True, they hadn't meant to kill Ariadne, but they had, and they daren't be found out. It wasn't so bad for Mrs. Davis, but for Vivienne it was almost unbearable. She had not only lost the sister she adored, but she had to pretend she didn't know any more about what had happened to her than anyone else. She also had to watch Doug's sorrow and pretend to sympathize with him. To her credit was the fact that she was so frightened and despondent that she wanted to withdraw from the coven. But they would not let her, and in time she was convinced that the beliefs of the witches would help her to carry on and overcome the horrible thing she and Mrs. Davis had done. So she threw herself into the coven with even more enthusiasm than she had before and in time was led to believe that what had happened was to her advantage. Now she was an entity in her own right and no longer a satellite of a gifted and beautiful sister as she had been all her life.

Rudy, although he had not been involved in Ariadne's death and did not know what had become of her, was considered one of the witches' coven and therefore forced to continue as one of them or be threatened with dire consequences. And Jason was in the same position. He didn't know what had happened to Ariadne but, especially after he lost his job with Doug, he was only too glad to be befriended by Vivienne. According to her, he had fallen in love with her, and being a weak character, he was easy for her to manipulate, especially since Mrs. Davis helped him get the drugs he had started taking.

The rest I knew, with the exception of the happenings on Sanctuary after my arrival. But these, too, came out during the merciless questioning of the police the night Vivienne and Rudy were arrested.

For instance, there was the identity of the goat man who presided over the coven the night Luke and I watched from behind a tree in the woods. To mine and Doug's surprise, it had been Jason. Jason, who no one knew was in any way connected with witchcraft. Only Luke had guessed, because of his discovery of Jason's association with Vivienne. I then remembered Jason's remark in the office the afternoon he had come in to pick up the material to take down to Vivienne's apartment, which of course had been material for two high priests' robes. He had said rather fervently, "I'm glad to do anything for Miss Vivienne."

It had been he, too, who had carried me from my room to the living room after Luke had brought me from the woods to my room when I fainted, because they wanted to scare me by putting Lisbeth's body in my bed. And it had been he who had left the robe and the goat's head on the bed in Doug's room, not knowing Doug would come back from Brussels so quickly; it had been the easiest way to dispose of it at the time.

It had also been he who had killed Lisbeth because she had threatened to tell about the covens and his and Vivienne's part in them. He hadn't wanted to, but the coven ordered him to, and he dared not disobey, or his supply of drugs would have been cut off. And it had been he who had put Lisbeth's body in my bed and later taken it away, also under orders of the coven. The body was found eventually, buried in a shallow grave back in the woods. It had also been Jason who had hit Luke on the back of the head and left him to drown at the edge of the lake, because he was becoming afraid Luke was getting too close to the truth.

When I told Luke the way Vivienne had acted the first day I had met her in the office, about the sparks in her eyes and the way she had backed away from me when I fingered the little silver cross I was wearing, he said, "Of course. They can't face the real truth of God."

It had been Vivienne who had painted the upside down cross in fluorescent paint on the mirror in my room at Sanctuary and it had been Vivienne who had taken all of Ariadne's clothes and personal possessions from her room on the island. She had keys to the entire place and had Doug's permission to go and come on the island as she pleased, so he really shouldn't have been annoyed that she was there the day I arrived.

Rudy had helped her replace Ariadne's piano in the living room with the electronically wired one that played by remote control from the next room, which was the guest room Vivienne used when she was on the island. It was explained to me in detail, but I am not mechanically inclined, so I didn't really understand it. Why they had gone to the trouble and expense of doing this wasn't quite clear. Something about trying to upset Doug and make him think it was Ariadne's ghost playing.

Thinking back, Doug, Luke and I were appalled at our lack of interest in investigating the other rooms in the complex when the grisly events were going on. But we were all so disturbed, I guess none of us thought very clearly, not even Luke.

Doug himself explained how he had come to disappear the time I had thought he was right behind me. He had thought he saw someone lurking behind the building that was my bedroom and had made a rush to grab whoever it was as quietly as he could, not even letting me know he was leaving me.

When I, in my desperation at finding myself alone on the path, had run back to the living room and found a goat man there, it had been Rudy. Luke had momentarily gone over to Doug's bedroom to wash up a little in his bathroom, and during that time Rudy, seeing the living room empty, had stopped in. Then I had returned and, seeing a goat man there, had fainted. And he had taken advantage of the situation to pick me up and take me back to the woods to be the virgin of the coven they were going to have.

It was after that that Luke and Doug had discovered I was missing, and Doug had decided to put on the black robe and goat's head that was still in his room and infiltrate the members of the coven to see what he could find out. That was how he and Luke had happened to be on hand to rescue me when I needed them later.

As to how Vivienne happened to be in the back of Doug's car, she reluctantly confessed to the police that when she read in the papers about Ariadne's body being found in the lake by Doug, she couldn't face the funeral. But she did go up to Pinecrest and stayed in a small boarding house on the lake, from which she had a view of the island of Sanctuary from her room. She registered under the name of May Craven, and no one recognized her.

That evening, thinking it was safe for her to go over to the inn for a drink, she had been sitting in a corner of the grill when Doug had telephoned the police. Seeing her opportunity to cause more trouble, she had managed to get out to the garage and hide in the back of Doug's car. The gun, she said, she always carried in her purse.

The rest was more or less like a bad dream, or rather a nightmare. Jason was picked up in New York, tried and found guilty and given twenty years to life. But because of his drug addiction, he was treated more like a sick man than a criminal and is in a mental hospital for treatment. Vivienne was convicted as an accessory, but on the examination of a psychiatrist was adjudged insane and was also put into a mental hospital for treatment.

Mrs. Davis had not been found. She had moved from her Chelsea apartment, leaving no address. The police, presumably, will not give up until they've found her. The other members of the coven, mostly artists, writers and musicians, were located, but there was nothing that could be held against them, so they were never brought to trial. It is not a criminal offense to be a witch, and as far as could be proved none of the rest of them had done any harm to anyone. No drugs were found on any of them or in their homes.

When it was all over, Doug immediately threw himself into his work, and I tried to do the same thing. But I couldn't seem to forget the things that had happened up at Sanctuary. Several times I caught Doug looking at me thoughtfully in the office, and I felt uncomfortable. I wondered if he had it in his mind to ask me to marry him after a suitable amount of time had elapsed, and I began to wonder what I would tell him. I hated to admit even to myself, but since we had returned to the city I hadn't heard any bells when he was near me. And try as I would, I couldn't keep from thinking of Luke.

With the mystery of Ariadne's disappearance solved, he had left Doug's employ and had returned to his profession of law. It seems the F.B.I. had arranged for him to work for Doug and act not only as an investigator of the mystery, but also as a bodyguard. But now that the F.B.I. had released him and Doug no longer needed him, he could once again be his own man.

Doug sold the limousine and bought a small sports car which he drove himself. And he had sold the island of Sanctuary and the entire complex to be used as a boys' summer camp.

One morning when I went into the office, I noticed that Ariadne's picture was gone from his desk. And it was that afternoon, while he was dictating some letters to me, that he stopped suddenly and, meeting my questioning eyes, asked, "Would you have dinner with me tonight? I think it is time we talked about our future together. Don't you?"

I felt my cheeks flushing, and my hands

began to perspire. I didn't know what to say. Once, an invitation like this from him would have sent me into seventh heaven, wherever that was. But now all I could feel was emptiness. Dining with Douglas Randolph, president of Amalgamated Fabrics, no longer held any joy for me.

When I didn't answer him right away, he asked, "Is it too soon?"

I shook my head and finally was able to speak. "It isn't that," I said. "It's — oh, I don't know just how to put it, but — well, I don't think you really want me as anything more than a secretary. You're just lonely."

He watched my face for a long moment before he said, "That's right. I am lonely. But not when I am with you. When I am with you, I feel a — well, call it a sort of peace. You understand me so well, far better than Ariadne ever did."

At the mention of her name, I couldn't help but shiver, and a cold feeling seemed to creep through me. "But you don't love me."

He gazed out the window at the steel and concrete towers of lower New York. "What is love?" he asked. "I thought I loved Ariadne. Now I'm not sure."

"Then how can you be sure you love me?"

He brought his gaze back to me, but there was still a far-away look in his eyes. "I didn't say I loved you. I said I needed you. Or that is what I was trying to say. In a way, that is love."

I got to my feet and discovered my knees were reluctant to hold me up, so I leaned against the end of the desk. "Perhaps I'd better hand in my resignation," I said, my voice as shaky as my knees.

The phone rang, and he reached for it. "Yes?" he said. Then, "Send him in, please."

I started to go to my office, but as he dropped the phone into place, he said, "Don't go."

I stopped, not knowing what to expect. He let me wait without saying anything more. In a moment the door opened and Luke walked in. To my surprise, my heart gave a jerk, then began to beat twice as fast as it normally did.

His eyes came directly to me. "Hello, Karen," he said.

Knowing my cheeks were beginning to redden, I said, "Hello, Luke."

With his eyes lingering on me, he said, "I hope I'm not interrupting anything important, Doug."

Doug said, "Not at all. Glad to see you. Sit down."

"I can't stay," Luke said. "I was just

passing by, and I thought I'd stop in and see if Karen was free for dinner tonight."

I gave Doug a quick glance. His face told me nothing, but he said, "Go ahead, if you want to." And I knew I was able to read more into those few words than Luke would be able to. But I couldn't help but hesitate. After all, Doug had meant so much to me for so long.

Seeing my hesitation, he said, "Go on. Get out of here, both of you. I have work to do."

So I nodded to Luke. "I'll get my things," I told him, and hurried into my office for my hat and purse. As I was putting on my hat before a small mirror I kept in my desk, I thought, Well, at least I won't have to grow a hyacinth plant and chant mumbo jumbo over it.

When I came out of my office, Luke and I said good night to Doug, and he said, "Good night. Have a pleasant evening."

A lump came into my throat, and I was glad to get out into the hall. As we hurried through the reception room, Alicia waved to us, and I saw her pick up a phone. I wondered if she was going to call Doug, knowing he was in the office alone. I shrugged mentally and thought, Well, so be it.

As we rode down in the elevator, Luke's and my eyes met, and I wondered if he was thinking the same thing I was. I was thinking that so far he'd never even kissed me. But I had the feeling that before the evening was over that state of affairs would change.

The employees of Thorndike Press hope you have enjoyed this Large Print book. All our Large Print titles are designed for easy reading, and all our books are made to last. Other Thorndike Press Large Print books are available at your library, through selected bookstores, or directly from the publishers.

For more information about titles, please call:

(800) 223-1244
   or
(800) 223-6121

To share your comments, please write:

Publisher
Thorndike Press
P.O. Box 159
Thorndike, Maine 04986